Ambushing an Ambush

Clint ran down the street toward the boardinghouse. When he came within sight of it, he could see Hannie standing on the street out front, waiting. Good, at least she hadn't gone rushing in.

Then he saw movement on one side of the house and quickened his pace.

Doyle snuck along the side of the house . . . and drew his gun. He had a clear view of Hannie, who was staring intently at the door. This was going to be easy.

As he aimed his gun at her, she was still staring ahead, flexing her fingers, waiting to draw her gun. This would be her last killing and then she'd take off the gun for good.

Getting closer to Hannie, Clint could see Doyle, cowardly planning on shooting her from ambush.

"Hannie! Watch out!" called Clint.

Hearing Clint's shout, Hannie didn't know which way to look, so she turned her back to look at him, giving Doyle a clear shot between her shoulder blades—and he cocked the hammer . . .

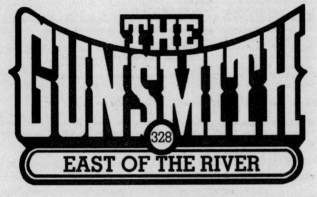

THE GUNSMITH

328

EAST OF THE RIVER

J. R. ROBERTS

JOVE BOOKS, NEW YORK

THE BERKLEY PUBLISHING GROUP
Published by the Penguin Group
Penguin Group (USA) Inc.
375 Hudson Street, New York, New York 10014, USA
Penguin Group (Canada), 90 Eglinton Avenue East, Suite 700, Toronto, Ontario M4P 2Y3, Canada
(a division of Pearson Penguin Canada Inc.)
Penguin Books Ltd., 80 Strand, London WC2R 0RL, England
Penguin Group Ireland, 25 St. Stephen's Green, Dublin 2, Ireland (a division of Penguin Books Ltd.)
Penguin Group (Australia), 250 Camberwell Road, Camberwell, Victoria 3124, Australia
(a division of Pearson Australia Group Pty. Ltd.)
Penguin Books India Pvt. Ltd., 11 Community Centre, Panchsheel Park, New Delhi—110 017, India
Penguin Group (NZ), 67 Apollo Drive, Rosedale, North Shore 0632, New Zealand
(a division of Pearson New Zealand Ltd.)
Penguin Books (South Africa) (Pty.) Ltd., 24 Sturdee Avenue, Rosebank, Johannesburg 2196,
South Africa

Penguin Books Ltd., Registered Offices: 80 Strand, London WC2R 0RL, England

This is a work of fiction. Names, characters, places, and incidents either are the product of the author's imagination or are used fictitiously, and any resemblance to actual persons, living or dead, business establishments, events, or locales is entirely coincidental.

EAST OF THE RIVER

A Jove Book / published by arrangement with the author

PRINTING HISTORY
Jove edition / April 2009

Copyright © 2009 by Robert J. Randisi.
Cover illustration by Sergio Giovine.

ISBN: 978-0-515-14608-0

JOVE®
Jove Books are published by The Berkley Publishing Group,
a division of Penguin Group (USA) Inc.,
375 Hudson Street, New York, New York 10014.
JOVE® is a registered trademark of Penguin Group (USA) Inc.
The "J" design is a trademark of Penguin Group (USA) Inc.

PRINTED IN THE UNITED STATES OF AMERICA

10   9   8   7   6   5   4   3   2   1

ONE

Clint Adams had admitted to himself a long time ago that he preferred life west of the Mississippi. Even when he went east, it was usually to St. Louis. This time, however, he was riding all the way to Indiana—to Marion County and, to be exact, the town of Ajax.

As he rode into town, he was unimpressed with Ajax. He wondered if the people who named the town knew anything about Greek mythology. Ajax the Great was the legendary king of Salamis Island, son of Telamon. But Ajax the Lesser was the son of King Oleus of Locris. Clint would have hated to be one of two Clints and described as "Clint the Lesser."

The only reason Clint knew this was that he read a lot, especially when he was on the trail. Mostly he read Dickens and Twain, but often he read history.

Ajax was a small town, but he'd been in smaller. The buildings were old, in disrepair, although in places you could see that someone had made an effort. There were some new boards here and there, and a couple of buildings with whole new walls, as if the old one had fallen and been replaced. But why anyone would pick this town for a poker game was beyond Clint.

He found the hotel—the only hotel in town, so why put a name on it other than "HOTEL"? This building was the newest in town, but that wasn't saying much. It seemed to be the only one that didn't look like a stiff wind would knock it over.

He dismounted, and wrapped Eclipse's reins carelessly around a hitching post as a formality. The horse would not go anywhere without him.

As he entered the hotel, he was surprised at the opulence he found. The furniture was plush; there was a crystal chandelier in the ceiling. The man standing behind the desk wore a black suit, his hair plastered down by some kind of hair tonic.

"Welcome to the Hotel, sir," the man said.

Clint approached the desk and said, "I'm looking for Harry Dial."

"Mr. Dial, the owner? Yes, sir. Can I say who—"

"Tell him Clint Adams is here."

"Clint Adams?" The clerk, a man probably in his thirties, suddenly got a lot younger. "Really? You mean . . . the Gunsmith?"

"Has anyone else arrived?"

"Anyone else?"

"You know, for the game."

"Oh, uh, the game," the clerk said. "Uh, no, sir, nobody's here."

"Okay, just tell Harry I'm here."

"Uh, sure, Mr. Adams, sure. Uh, Mr. Dial is in his room, room one? I'll go up and—"

"Is he alone?"

"Uh, no, sir."

"Who's with him?"

"Well, uh . . ."

"A woman?"

The clerk grinned and said, "Yes, sir. I'll just go and tell him—"

"That's okay," Clint said, putting his hand on the man's arm, "I'll announce myself."

"Uh, yes, sir, it's, uh, up one flight."

Clint turned and went to the stairs.

Harry Dial flipped the blonde over onto her belly and filled his hands with the cheeks of her ample butt. He loved girls with big butts, and Sophie had the biggest of all the girls who worked at the cathouse.

"Ooh," she moaned, "you're gonna leave marks on my ass, Harry."

"That ain't all I'm gonna leave," he growled.

He lifted her up so she was on all fours, then spread her cheeks and pressed his rigid penis against her—

The knock on the door interrupted him.

"Go away!"

The knock became a pounding.

"Jesus!" he said, getting off the bed. "Don't go anywhere, Sophie."

Sophie turned and sat, and said, "Where would I go, Harry? You're payin' me for my time."

"Yeah," he said, walking to the door, "just remember that, girl. I'm payin' you for your time . . . and your ass!"

"Haw, Harry!" she said. "You're such a romantic!"

Harry opened the door wide, stood there naked, and shouted, "What?"

"Let's play cards, Harry," Clint Adams said.

TWO

"What do you mean nobody's coming?" Clint demanded.

The blonde on the bed had had such large, pale breasts that Clint had been momentarily stunned into silence. He couldn't take his eyes off her large, pink nipples.

"Clint!"

Dial saying his name had broken the spell.

"Harry, what's going on?" he'd asked.

"Jesus, Clint, I tried to get ahold of you. I sent telegrams, but I guess none of them ever caught up to you. So I just figured I'd tell you when you got here."

"Tell me what, Harry?"

"Look," Dial said, "let me get dressed and meet you in the lobby. Huh? Two minutes."

Harry's erection had wilted, so Clint was pretty sure he was only going to use the two minutes to get dressed.

"Okay, Harry," he said, "two minutes." He looked at the woman. "Ma'am, sorry to interrupt."

He turned and went down to the lobby. Exactly

two minutes later Harry appeared, fully dressed, and took Clint across the street to the saloon, where they were now, seated at a table with a beer each.

"Harry?"

Dial had just told Clint that none of the other players were coming.

"Like I said," Dial repeated, "they can't come. They canceled."

"All of them?"

"Well, a few," Dial admitted, "but when I got the telegrams with the cancellations, I figured, why go ahead with the whole thing? There wouldn't be enough money to make it worth anyone's while."

"So you sent telegrams to everyone, telling them not to come?"

Dial shrugged and said, "Well, yeah, it seemed the right thing to do."

"Except for me."

Dial again shrugged his big shoulders. He was built like a bear, and since Clint had seen him naked, he knew that the man had almost as much hair all over his body. He tried to block the picture out of his mind, replace it with the naked woman on the bed.

"I told you, I tried to get hold of you, Clint," Dial said. "I really did!"

Clint had been on the trail for at least two weeks, so if he gave the man the benefit of the doubt, he couldn't really fault him.

"Crap," he said, sitting back heavily in his chair, "What the hell am I going to do in this hole without that game?"

"Well . . . we do have a cathouse."

"I don't pay for girls, Harry," Clint said.

"I forgot that," Dial said. "Well, I could pay—"

"No," Clint said, "That's okay, Harry. Don't worry about it."

"Well, I feel responsible for you coming all this way for nothin'," Dial said.

"That's because you are responsible," Clint pointed out.

"Yeah, well . . ." Dial shrugged.

"Okay," Clint said, "I'll get a night's sleep and head out in the morning."

"For where?" Harry asked.

"I don't know," Clint said. "St. Louis, I guess, and then across the river. Unless you know of another game taking place somewhere?"

"Not east of the Mississippi."

"See?" Clint said. "I knew nothing good could come from crossing to this side of the river."

"What's wrong with this side of the river?" Dial demanded.

"Oh, nothing much," Clint said, "except that it's east."

"Now, wait—"

"No offense meant, Harry," Clint said.

"Really? How the hell could I possibly not take offense at that?"

"Can I get a good steak in this town?"

"Yes," Dial said, "I can take you someplace for a good steak, but first I have to go and finish what I started."

"What's tha— Oh, right," Clint said. "I interrupted you."

"Come back to the hotel with me," Dial said, standing up. "We'll get you a room. After that you can see to your horse. And by that time I should be ready to take you for that steak."

"Okay," Clint said, standing, "but I'm telling you now, it's going to have to be one hell of a steak to make this trip worth it."

"I said it would be a good steak," Dial said. "But that good? I don't know."

THREE

Twenty miles away, in the town of Dexter, Indiana, young Sam Archer entered the family general store. He was wearing his hat cocked at a rakish angle and his gun too low on his thigh.

His older brother, Thomas, was waiting on two middle-aged women while his other older brother, John, was in the storeroom. The oldest of the four brothers, Mort, was out at their farm, which was on the outskirts of town, in Orange County, while the store was in Marion County.

As the two women left with their purchases, Thomas looked at his brother and asked, "What are you supposed to be?"

"Whataya mean?"

"That hat," Thomas said. "Straighten it out."

"What?" Sam asked. He went to a mirror on the wall by the new hats. "I like it like this."

"It looks stupid."

"It does not!"

"Let's get a neutral opinion," Thomas Archer said. "John?"

Sam turned to see his brother John entering the room from the back.

"What?"

"What do you think of the way little brother's wearin' his hat?"

John looked at Sam and said, "It's stupid."

"It is not!"

"And what's with that gun?" John asked.

"What's wrong with my gun?" Sam demanded.

"It's too low," Thomas said.

"I wear it there for a fast draw."

"What do you need with a fast draw?" Thomas asked.

"And when did you get one?" John asked.

"Come on," Sam said, "you know I'm fast."

John looked around, making sure the store was empty before he continued.

"Little brother, for what we do you don't need a fast draw."

"Besides," Thomas said, sliding a pencil behind his ear, "either one of us could pick up any gun in this store and outdraw you with it."

"You could not!"

"Yeah," John said, "we could. What are you doin' here, kid?"

"Mort sent me for supplies."

"Where's the wagon?" John asked.

"In front."

"Well, pull the damn thing around back and load up," Thomas said.

Sam looked in the mirror again, uncocked the hat, then recocked it and walked out the door. John walked over to where Thomas was standing behind the counter. Both men were wearing white aprons.

John looked around carefully to make sure they were alone before he spoke.

"We're gettin' short," he said.

"How short?" Thomas asked.

"That depends on how much Sam takes back to the farm with him."

"Then I guess it's time for us to go out again," Thomas said.

"Yeah."

"Time to talk to Mort."

John leaned on the counter. "I'm gettin' real tired of havin' to check with Mort every time this comes up."

"He is the oldest, John," Thomas said. "And this is a family business."

"Yeah," John said, "I know. Okay, I'm gonna go in the back and help little brother load up, then I'll saddle up and ride out to talk to Mort."

"Fine," Thomas said. "I'll hold down the fort here."

Mort Archer heard his brothers approaching before he saw them. He stepped outside onto the porch and saw Sam driving the wagon and John riding his horse. There was only one reason John would be coming out to the farm this early in the day.

He stepped off the porch and started walking toward them.

John saw Mort step down off the porch.

"Sam!" he shouted. "Unload in the barn first."

Sam nodded and turned the team toward the barn. John continued to ride toward his other brother.

"Is it time?" Mort asked as John dismounted.

"Yeah, big brother," John said. "It's time."

"Okay," Mort said. "Come inside and let's talk."

FOUR

Harry Dial had been right about the steak. It was good, but it was not worth the long ride. Clint sat back and patted his stomach.

"You feelin' better?" Dial asked.

"A little," Clint said. "Okay, I know it's not your fault, but I rode a long way for nothing."

"I understand that," Dial said, "and I'm sorry. I can probably scare up a game for you."

"I'm not interested in a pickup game," Clint said. "I was in the mood for some serious poker."

"Well . . . there is a place you might find a game," Dial said.

"Oh? Where?"

"Dexter."

"What's Dexter?"

"A town in the neighboring county," Dial said. "We're in Marion. Dexter's in Orange County."

"Big town?"

"Bigger than this one."

"That isn't saying much."

"It's big enough," Dial said. "Got everything you'd need to salvage the trip."

"Is that right?"

"Coupla saloons, with girls and games, some restaurants, two hotels . . ."

"Sounds like any other town."

"Go to the Ox Bow Saloon," Dial told him. "Talk to Eddie Randle. If there are gamblers in town, he'll know. Say, since when did you become a big gambler?"

"When a good game comes around, I'm interested," Clint said. "Wasn't Bat Masterson supposed to be here?"

"Bat was the first one to cancel," Dial said. "Ran into some trouble."

"What kind of trouble?"

"Nothin' he couldn't handle," Dial said. "At least, that's what his telegram said."

"Bat thinks he can handle anything—and he usually can," Clint said.

They got up, paid the bill, and left.

"What are you going to do now?" Dial asked.

"Check on my horse," Clint said. "Then I guess I'll go to my room."

"Come by my place first," Dial said. "I'll give you a couple of beers on the house."

"You got a deal."

Clint made sure Eclipse was fed and bedded down for the night, then went over to the saloon. Dial was waiting for him at the bar.

"Paul, a beer for Mr. Adams," he said. "On the house, followed by a second."

"Yes, sir."

"And bring me one."

Clint picked up his beer and took a couple of swallows. It was ice cold. He looked around. The place was almost empty.

"What are you doing here, Harry?" he asked.

"Here? This is my place."

"You own the hotel, too?"

"Yup."

"Why?" Clint asked. "This town looks like it'll blow away soon."

"I'm doin' okay here, Clint," Dial said. "The town's gonna come back."

"You really think so?"

"I'm gonna make it come back."

"How much of it do you own?"

"About half," Dial said. "Nobody else wanted it."

"Why do you want it?"

Dial shrugged.

"I rode in here one day and just about the whole place was up for grabs," Dial said. "I guess I saw a chance to own my own town."

"And do what with it? Die?"

"We won't die," Dial said. "I'm gonna have a few of these games every month. It'll help me raise the money I need to fix this place up."

"Where are you going to get your supplies?"

"Well, until I can get the general store up and running again, I'll go to Dexter. The Archer boys have a general store there."

"Archer?"

"Four brothers," Dial said. "They run the store, and they have a farm outside of town."

"Well, I wish you luck, Harry," Clint said. "I think you're going to need it."

"You make your own luck, Clint," Dial said. "That's what I'm tryin' to do."

Clint finished his beer and set the mug down.

"What about that second one?"

"Next time," Clint said, although once he left Ajax, Indiana, he knew he'd never be back.

FIVE

"We'll take the kid with us," Mort said.

"What?" John asked.

"Sam," Mort said.

"I know who the kid is, Mort," John said. "Why would we take him with us?"

"It's time for him to learn the family business, don't you think?"

"Why?"

"Well, for one thing he wants to," Mort said. "He's been askin' me when he can go."

"Sam's eighteen, Mort."

"He's a man," Mort said. "And he's got to pull his weight."

"So put him to work here."

"On the farm?" Mort asked. "Sam's no farmer. Believe me, I've tried. Just like you and Thomas."

"We have to run the store."

"And the farm gets run into the ground."

"Mort," John said, "we can give up the farm."

"No," Mort said, "we need it. It's a good cover."

"So's the store."

"As long as we're farmers and storekeepers," Mort said, "nobody's gonna think we're also bank and train robbers."

"Not to mention stagecoaches."

"Yeah," Mort said, "them, too."

Sam came busting in the front door carrying a box of supplies.

"I got everything put away in the barn, Mort," he said, putting the box on the table. "Here's the rest of it."

"Put it all away, kid."

"But, Mort, I wanna go back to town."

"Not yet," Mort said. "John and me are talkin' about our next job."

"We got a job comin' up?" Sam asked, excited.

"That's right."

"You said I could go on the next one, Mort," Sam said. He looked at John. "That's what he said, John."

"I know it."

"What's the job?" Sam asked.

"We haven't decided yet," Mort said. "We'll have to talk to Tom about it, too."

"I can ride into town and get 'im."

"Don't worry," John said. "He'll be here as soon as he closes up. He knows we're gonna talk about this tonight."

"You got somethin' in mind?" Mort asked John.

"We could hit the bank in Munro," John said.

"We hit that bank already."

"Yeah, but it's the biggest one in the county," John said. "We'll just have to do the one job. Why? You got any ideas?"

"I was thinkin' about somethin' we never done before," Mort said.

"Like what?"

"Like hittin' two stagecoaches at the same time."

"Yeah, that is somethin' we never done before," John said, "with good reason."

"Right," Mort said, "because there was only three of us, but now we're four."

"That's right!" Sam said.

"You're supposed to put the rest of the supplies away, Sammy," Mort said.

"Yeah, sure, Mort."

"Two stagecoaches," John said.

"That idea appeal to you, Johnny?"

"Yeah, kinda," John said, "but I don't know if it'll appeal to Tom."

"You let me worry about Tommy."

Thomas Archer came out the front door of the store and locked it behind him. When he turned, he came face-to-face with the law.

"Hey, Sheriff."

"Tom," Sheriff Lou Perry said. "Closin' up early for the day?"

"Yeah," Thomas said, "gotta go out to the farm and help Mort."

"You fellas sure are hard workers," Perry said. "Hell, you're my age, Tom. Farmin' and storekeepin', that's hard work."

"We ain't exactly old, Sheriff, are we?" Thomas asked.

"Forty," Perry said, "forty's pretty old. In fact, I been feelin' kind of old lately."

"Yeah, well, just think about Mort," Thomas said. "Poor guy's forty-five."

"Yeah," the sheriff said, "I guess things could always be worse, right?"

"You got that right, Sheriff," Thomas said. "Things could always be worse."

SIX

Clint was about to reread Mark Twain's *Adventures of Huckleberry Finn* when there was a knock at the door. He was rereading the book because Twain had not come out with a new one since its publication in 1884. He'd exchanged some letters with Twain where the man said he was working on something that had to do with King Arthur. Clint couldn't wait to read that one.

He put *Finn* down on the rickety night table and took his gun from the holster that was hanging on the bedpost. He carried the gun to the door with him.

"Who is it?"

A woman's voice said, "Harry sent me."

"Harry . . . ," Clint said, shaking his head.

He was still cautious as he opened the door, gun ready. Standing in the hall was the big-breasted, pale-skinned blonde who had been in bed with Harry earlier in the day.

"Remember me?" she asked, with a smile.

"Listen," Clint said, "tell Harry I appreciate the thought but—"

"—you don't pay for whores," she finished for him. "I know, I heard. But I'm not here as a whore."

"What are you here as?" he asked.

"A woman," she said, "one who really doesn't like standing in the hall."

"What's your name?"

"Sophie."

"Sophie," he said, "you're a lovely girl—"

She laughed.

"I ain't been a girl in a long time, Mr. Adams," she said, "and I also ain't been lovely, but I do have these." She took hold of the front of her dress and pulled it down so that her bare breasts fell out. Her pink nipples were hard.

"You kind of noticed them this afternoon, didn't you?" she asked.

"How could I not?"

"So?" she asked. "Do you want to leave me out here in the hall with my breasts hangin' out?"

"No," he said, "no, of course not. Get in here."

He opened the door, backed up so she could enter, then closed it. By the time he turned to face her, she had her breasts covered.

"Hello," she said.

"Hello," he said.

She saw the gun in his hand.

"Sorry," he said. He walked to the bedpost and holstered the gun. "Can't be too careful."

"I understand," she said. "Harry told me who you are. Clint Adams, the Gunsmith. This is quite an honor."

"Is it?"

"You're very famous," she said. "I've never met a famous person before."

"I'm afraid I'm just like anyone else."

She walked toward him. He was suddenly aware of the fact that he was half naked, his torso and feet bare. And the dress she was wearing was thin cotton, clinging to her lush body like a second skin. And she'd already proven how quickly she could take at least part of it off.

She came close to him, and he could feel the heat her body gave off, and smell the scent of her sex.

His body reacted naturally, and there was nothing he could do about it.

When she got close enough to touch him, she did. She placed her hand on his crotch, felt how swollen he was.

"Ooh," she said, "not just like anybody else, I see."

"Sophie—"

"Shh," she said, reaching for his belt. "I'm not askin' for any money, Clint. Can I call you Clint?"

"Sure," he said, his mouth going dry.

"Harry said you had nothin' to do tonight," she told him, "said you were leavin' in the mornin'. All I want is a little bit of your time."

"My time?"

She slid off his belt, undid the button on his trousers.

"One night, then," she said. "One for both of us to remember."

She reached into his pants, inside his underwear, to take hold of his swollen cock.

"Ooh," she said, "you're hot."

"So are you," he said. "It's coming off you in waves."

"I know," she said, lowering her voice and licking her bottom lip. "I get like that. Men have commented on it before."

She stroked him inside his pants.

"I'm gonna take this out of your pants now," she said. "You can stop me if you want."

He reached out, hooked his finger inside the front of her dress, and pulled it down until her breasts spilled out.

"I don't think I want to stop you."

SEVEN

She lowered Clint's pants and shorts to the floor, and his erection popped free.

"Ooh," she said, getting down on her knees.

She took him in both hands, licked the head of his penis until it was very wet, then slid it into her mouth. She began to suck on him and, at the same time, stroke him with one hand.

"Jesus," he said.

Her wet mouth took more and more of him in, until, at one point, she had his entire length in her mouth. She held him there for a moment, then released and gasped, catching her breath.

"Jesus," she said, "you could choke a girl."

"I wouldn't want to do that," he said. He reached down, pulled her to her feet, then hastily removed her dress, peeling it off of her. When she was completely naked, he stepped back so he could look at her. She had a fleshy body—big breasts, wide hips, strong thighs and calves. She was a large woman, not fat—not yet anyway. In her later years she'd probably go that way, but at the moment she was mouthwatering.

He moved closer, took her breasts into his palms, and hefted them.

"I know," she said, "they're heavy, but you don't have to carry them around all day."

"Well," he said, thumbing her nipples, "you might have complaints, but I don't."

He lifted her breasts to his mouth, sucked each nipple until it was very hard, then bit them.

"Oooh, yeah," she said, "bite 'em hard."

While he sucked her breasts, she reached down and stroked his dick.

"God, it's gettin' even bigger," she marveled.

"So are your nipples."

"I know," she said. "Sometimes I think they're so ugly."

"Ugly?" He stared at her. "Are we looking at the same nipples? They're a beautiful pink."

"But they're so big."

"Makes it easier to bite them," he said, demonstrating.

"Ouch."

"Sorry."

"No, it's fine," she said, "but how would you like me to bite you?"

He smiled and said, "Yes, please."

She got on her knees again and began to nibble on him. Eventually, though, her tongue came out and she started licking up and down the length of him—up one side, down the other. While she sucked him, he reached down to cup her breasts, tweaking her nipples. Then he put his hands in her armpits and lifted her to her feet.

"Time for the bed," he said.

"What's the hurry, big boy?" she asked with a smile. "We got all night."

"You're making my legs weak."

"Ain't you sweet," she said, then licked her lips and added. "Well, yeah, you are. Come on, I wanna suck some more on that salt lick of yours."

He pulled her to him for a deep kiss, and walked her to the bed while still in the clinch. When they fell onto the bed together, she once again maneuvered herself between his legs and began to suck on him. Lying on his back, he put his hands up over his head and began to move his hips in unison with her mouth, so that eventually he was fucking her mouth.

"Mmm, mmm," she moaned, digging her nails into his thighs.

Just when he thought he couldn't take any more, she release him and gripped his penis tightly at the base to ward off his orgasm.

"See that?" she asked. "I'm an expert. I could keep this up all night."

He took a deep breath and said, "Lucky me . . ."

It was the most exquisite torture he'd ever endured. She would suck him for what felt like hours, and refuse to let him climax. Finally, though, she allowed him to explode into her mouth. He cried out, lifted his butt off the bed, and let loose. He flopped around until she had sucked him dry; then she released him and settled back onto her haunches, grinning at him while he tried to catch his breath.

"That was . . . That was . . . ," he said.

"Memorable?"

"To say the least."

"Think you can match that?" she asked. "And please remember, I'm a professional."

"That's okay," he said. "I've been doing this for a long time, too."

"Okay, then," she said, settling down onto her butt and spreading her legs, "get to it, mister."

EIGHT

The Archer brothers talked all evening, even while Mort cooked dinner and they all sat at the kitchen table, eating.

"I like Mort's idea," Sam said. "Two stages in one day."

"Or two banks," Mort said. "Either one."

"You ain't got much of a say, Sam," Thomas said. He wasn't all that happy when he got to the farm and discovered that Mort and John had agreed that Sam would be part of the gang now.

"He's our brother," John said. "It stands to reason he'd be part of the gang."

"I suppose . . ."

"So that means I get an opinion, right?" Sam asked. "Right, Mort?"

"Right, Sammy," Mort said. "You get an opinion."

"Then I agree with you," the kid said. "Two jobs in one day."

"It makes a statement," Mort said.

"And maybe makes us enough money that we won't have to pull another job for a while," John said.

"Well," Thomas said. "that ain't gonna happen with two stagecoaches, unless we hit one that's carrying a payroll."

"So then that means two banks," John said.

"But not banks that we've already hit," Mort said.

"How about one in Orange County, and one in Marion?" John asked.

"Sounds good to me," Sam said anxiously.

"Okay then," Mort said, carrying the plates to the sink, "then we gotta decide which two banks in which two towns."

"What about Ajax?" Sam asked. He remembered being there once and going to the cathouse.

"You just wanna go see that big blonde that made a man outta you," John said.

"Sophie, wasn't that her name?" Thomas asked.

"Yeah, that was her!" Sam said, his eyes shining.

"Boy," Mort said, "you gotta learn the difference between business and pleasure. We're either gonna rob a bank or get our ashes hauled, but we can't do both."

"Yeah, get it together, boy," Thomas said.

"Sam, why don't you go out and check on the horses?" John said.

"Aw, Johnny—"

"Don't worry," John said, "we're not gonna make any decisions while you're outside."

"Oh, all right."

Sam went out the door.

"He ain't ready," Thomas said.

"What makes you say that?" Mort asked.

"'Cause we're talkin' about robbin' banks and he's talkin' about some whore's cunny, that's why."

"Hell, Tommy," Mort said, "seems to me when you was his age all you thought about was pokin' some whore."

"Yeah," John said, "remember that time in Abilene—"

"Forget that time in Abilene," Thomas said. "When I was Sam's age, I was smarter and more mature."

"Well," John said, "how are we gonna know if he's ready if we don't take him with us?"

"Yeah, but this two-job idea," Thomas said, "why don't we wait on that until we know we can trust him?"

"You wanna wait?" John asked. "We need some operating capital now, brother."

"No, I don't mean to wait," Thomas said. "I mean let's pick one job—a stage, a bank—and see how little brother does under pressure."

"Johnny?" Mort asked.

"I say let's go with the two jobs, Mort," John said. "I think Sam'll do fine."

"So I guess that leaves the decision up to me," Mort said.

"What about Sam?" John asked. "He gets a vote."

"What do you think he'll vote?" Thomas asked sarcastically.

"We'll give him a vote," Mort said, "but I'll still make the final decision."

"When?" Thomas asked.

"Tomorrow," Mort said. "I'll make up my mind tomorrow."

"About what?" John asked. "Which job, or if Sam gets to come along?"

"I'll decide whether or not Sammy comes," Mort

said, "and then we'll all decide on the job. How's that?"

"That works for me," John said.

"Tommy?" Mort said.

"Yeah, sure," Thomas said. "Why not? We got any coffee, Mort?"

"Coffee," Mort said, "and I made an apple pie."

"Mom's apple pie?" John asked.

"Who else's recipe would I have?" the older brother replied.

NINE

Sophie was beating her fists on the mattress, tossing her head from side to side as Clint licked her pussy, teased her with his tongue and lips, even nibbled on her, until she reached down to grab his head in her hands.

"Stop stop, you're killin' me," she gasped. "T-too much! Too good."

He looked up at her from between her meaty thighs and grinned.

"How can there be too much pleasure?"

Gasping for air, she said, "I didn't think there could be, but I was wrong. You're good, Clint. Now, why don't you just get up here and stick that thing in me like you're supposed to."

"You don't have to ask me twice."

His penis was red and pulsing as he mounted her, pressed against her wet pussy, and then slid in easily to the hilt. She gasped, her eyes going wide, then locked her strong legs around his hips as he began to fuck her . . .

• • •

Later they lay together on the bed, her head on his shoulder. She had his penis in her hand and he had an arm around her, his hand clasped to one big breast.

"My God," she said, "you took me at my word, didn't you?"

"What was that?"

"That we should have us a night to remember?"

He rolled her nipple with his fingers and said, "Far as I can see, the night's not over yet."

"Are you serious?"

"I thought you were serious," Clint said. "You mean you're all talk?"

She started to laugh. "I think I've already proved to you that I ain't all talk, cowboy."

The nipple between his fingers grew hard and chewable.

"Yeah," he said. "I think I can see that."

He began to grow erect in her hand, and she said, "I can see it, too."

"Going to be a long, hard . . . pretty enjoyable night."

It was all that.

Long . . .

Hard . . .

Enjoyable . . .

They both woke the next morning exhausted.

"Are you still leaving this mornin'?" she asked, stretching.

"Oh yeah," he said, rolling over.

She was on her back, and stretching pulled her big, beautiful breasts taut. He reached over and cupped one in his hand.

"I don't believe it," she said.

He slid his hand down over her belly until he was cupping her gold pubic thatch. He delved in with his middle finger and touched her.

"Believe it," he said . . .

"Okay, okay," she gasped, rolling away from him sometime later, "you win . . . When are you leavin'?"

"Right after breakfast."

"Breakfast?"

"You want to eat with me?"

"I can't eat," she said, pressing her face into a pillow. "I'm too tired."

"Well then," he said, swinging his feet to the floor, "you stay here as long as you want. I need to have breakfast if I'm going to hit the trail."

"Where are you heading?"

"Harry told me about a town called Dexter."

"Well, that's not a very long ride," she said.

"You saying you don't want me to leave yet?" he asked.

"Well, you could stay awhile."

"Another hour?"

"Are you crazy?" she asked. "I was thinking more like another day or so."

"Sorry," he said, getting up. "I've got to go."

"Well, I'm real sorry, then," she told him, "but I don't have another hour in me."

He didn't want to tell her that neither did he.

Thomas and John spent the night on the farm, even though they both had rooms in town.

"You really think the kid is ready?" Thomas asked.

"I think we're gonna find out," John said.

"Yeah," Thomas said, "as soon as we pick out a target. You got one in mind?"

"No."

"Me, neither," Thomas said. "I guess we should just open the store and leave that to Mort, huh?"

"Hey," John said with a shrug, "he's the big brother."

Clint walked to the livery after breakfast to retrieve Eclipse. As he walked him out, Harry Dial appeared.

"How was your night?" Dial asked.

"Great," Clint said. "How was yours?"

"Quiet."

"What are you doing here?"

"I just wanted to apologize again for not bein' able to reach you."

"Forget it, Harry," Clint said. "I'll check out Dexter and then head west."

"I hope you find a game and make some money," Dial said. "Maybe even enough to make the trip worth your while."

"I'll check it out, Harry," Clint said, mounting up. "Listen, if you do manage to get another game together?"

"Yeah?"

"Don't count on me."

TEN

As he rode into Dexter, Clint could see it was ten times the size of Ajax. Which wasn't saying much, but at least it was a town.

Riding down Main Street, he passed everything Harry Dial had told him was there. Two saloons, two hotels—unimaginatively called the Hotel Dexter and the Dexter Hotel—a few cafés, a bank . . . he even rode past the sheriff's office. Eventually, he found his way to the livery.

"That's some animal," the old liveryman said.

"Yes, he is," Clint said. "He needs very special handling, though. Might take your finger off."

"I think I can handle him," the man said. He held up his left hand, which was missing parts of the last two fingers. "I'm already missing some fingers."

"I can see that," Clint said. "Okay, he's all yours."

The man accepted the reins and said, "I'll take good care of him."

Clint handed the man a dollar and said, "See that you do."

"Okay."

"I see this town's got two hotels," Clint said. "Which one is the best?"

"Try the Hotel Dexter."

"Thanks."

Clint took his rifle and saddlebags and walked to the hotel.

John Archer opened the front door to allow a couple of waiting customers to come in.

"You're opening a little late today, John," a sixty-ish woman said.

"Sorry, Mrs. Weston," he said. "We had to go out to the farm last night."

"How are things on the farm?" she asked. "How is Mort?"

"The farm's fine, and so is Mort."

"Your mother would be so proud of you boys."

"I hope you're right, ma'am."

"Hello, Thomas," Mrs. Weston said, approaching the desk. "I have a list."

The other customer was a man called Doyle.

"What are you doin' here?" John asked him, keeping his voice low.

"I was just wonderin' if you had any work, Johnny," Doyle said. "You know? Work?"

"You wanna push a broom around in here, Doyle?" John asked.

Doyle, in his thirties, had a heavy beard, which was his effort to hide a homely face. Now he scratched it, and John swore he saw a couple of bugs—maybe lice—jump out.

"That wasn't the kind of work I had in mind, Johnny," Doyle said.

"Well, that's all we got right now," John said. "Unless you wanna go out and work on the farm. Been behind a plow lately?"

"Come on, Johnny," Doyle said. "I'm talkin' about a job—"

"Keep your voice down!" John hissed. "As far as the people in this town know, we're legit town businessmen and farmers."

"Okay, okay."

"Where are you stayin'?" John asked.

"The Dexter Hotel."

"You sure? There's two—"

"Wha— Oh yeah, what's that about? People in this town got no imagination?"

"None," John said. "Wait at your hotel. We'll be in touch."

"All right," Doyle said. "Thanks. I knew I could count on you."

"And don't come back here," John said, pushing the man out the door.

As he turned around, Thomas gave him a questioning look from behind the counter. John shrugged, mouthed "Later," and Thomas went back to filling Mrs. Weston's list.

Clint checked into the hotel, left his rifle and saddlebags there, and went back down to talk to the clerk.

"Good steak," he said. "Where can I find one?"

"Across the street," the man said. "Small café. Don't look like much, but good food."

Clint put a dollar in the man's hand and said, "Thanks."

Clint left the hotel and saw the café across the street, but before checking that out, he walked down the street toward the Ox Bow Saloon.

ELEVEN

It was afternoon as he entered the saloon, and the place was about half filled. The gaming tables were still covered, though, and it was too early for any girls to be working the floor.

He approached the bar. Several men standing there turned to watch him.

"Help ya?" one of them asked.

"Are you Eddie Randle?"

"No."

"Then you can't help me."

He called the bartender over.

"What can I do for you, friend?"

"He ain't very friendly, Newly," the other man told the bartender.

"Maybe he just don't wanna talk to a loser like you, Harvey."

"Hey, wha the—"

"Just shut up, Harve," the bartender said, and looked at Clint again. "What can I do for you, fella?"

"I'm looking for Eddie Randle."

"Mr. Randle owns this place," the bartender said. "Does he know you?"

"No," Clint said, "but he knows Harry Dial."

"Hell," the bartender said, "I know Harry Dial." He extended his hand. "My name's Newly Hagen."

"Clint Adams."

"Whoa, the Gunsmith?" Hagen said as they shook hands.

"Hey, Mr. Adams," the other man said suddenly. "I didn't mean nothin'—"

"Shut up, Harve!" Hagen said. "Come on, Mr. Adams. I'll take you to Eddie."

Clint followed the bartender along the length of the bar until the man came out from behind it. There must have been a platform behind it, for as Clint followed him across the floor, he realized that Hagen was barely five-foot-six.

They went to an office door in the back and Hagen knocked.

"Eddie, got somebody here wants to—" He stopped short.

Clint entered the office behind the diminutive bartender. It was empty.

"Huh," Hagen said. "He was here a minute ago."

"Where does that door lead?" Clint asked, pointing to a door in the back wall.

"Storeroom."

"And beyond that?"

"An alley in the back."

"Does he go out that way?"

"Sometimes."

"So okay," Clint said. "I guess I'll meet him later."

"You want a beer while you wait?"

"What I want is a steak," Clint said. "The clerk at the hotel told me about a place across the street."

"Across the street? From which place?"

"The Hotel Dexter."

"Yeah, that café is good," Hagen confirmed.

"Okay," Clint said, "then I'll go and have a steak and then come back for that beer. Maybe Eddie will be here by then."

"He's usually back to take the covers off the tables," Hagen said.

"Good."

They left the office, returned to the saloon, and walked to the bar. The men who had been standing there when Clint entered were gone.

"Sorry if I scared away your customers."

"Harve and his idiot friends? They can nurse the hell out of one beer. Good riddance."

TWELVE

Eddie Randle entered Archer's General Store, stopped just inside, looked around, and then approached the counter.

"Eddie," Thomas said.

"I just need a few things, Tom," Randle said. He handed Thomas a list.

"We can handle all of this," Thomas said. "How's business?"

"Great," Randle said. "Business is pickin' up, in fact."

"Really?"

"How about you?" Randle asked. "How's business in here?"

"Oh, pretty good."

"And the farm?" Randle asked. "How are things goin' out there?"

"Just fine, Eddie," Thomas said.

"More and more people movin' to town, Thomas," Randle said, shaking his head. "Our population is growin'. Pretty soon, we're gonna need another bank."

"Two banks?"

"Lots of towns have two banks, Thomas," Randle said.

"Yeah, I know that," Thomas said. "Just didn't figure this would ever be one of 'em."

"And towns with two banks, they need more law than most," Randle said.

"I guess so," Thomas said thoughtfully. "Let me fill this list for ya and get ya on your way, Eddie."

"Thanks, Tom."

Randle looked around again, didn't see any sign of John. Then he heard some noise from the back room, figured the other brother must be there.

The shelves didn't look as well stocked as they might have. That could mean that business was good, or that the boys didn't have the cash to restock.

He wondered which it was.

The steak wasn't as good as the one Clint had had in the small town of Ajax, but it got rid of the hunger pangs. Over a pot of coffee, he once again lamented ths fact that he had ridden a long way from Texas for no reason. Now he was just flailing around, trying to find something to make the trip worth it. It didn't feel good, or right. What he probably should have been doing was mounting up and heading west.

But while he was here, he figured he might as well meet Eddie Randle and see what Harry Dial's friend had to offer, if anything.

He paid his bill, left the café, and walked back to the Ox Bow Saloon.

• • •

When Eddie Randle came walking into the Ox Bow carrying a box, Newly Hagen hurriedly followed him to his office.

"What's on your mind, Newly?" Randle asked, putting the box down on his desk.

"Fella was here lookin' for you a little while ago," the bartender said.

"I owe him money, or he owe me money?"

"No, nothing like that," Hagen said. "He's a friend of Harry Dial's."

"I heard Harry had to cancel his big game," Randle said. "Could this be one of the players?"

"You tell me," Hagen said. "It's Clint Adams."

"He don't have a reputation for cards," Randle commented.

"Well, he was lookin' for you."

"When he comes back, bring him in to see me," Randle said. "Might as well see what he wants."

"You ain't done nothin' to make him mad, have ya, Eddie? Or Harry Dial?"

"You think Harry Dial sent the Gunsmith here to kill me?" Randle asked. "That's crazy. No, I ain't done nothin' to either of 'em. Just bring 'im in to see me, Newly."

"Okay."

"Now get outta here and go to work."

"Yup."

Newly Hagen turned and went out the door, closing it firmly behind him.

As Hagen left, Randle walked around and sat behind his desk. He got out a cigar, clipped the end, and lit it up, then leaned back in his chair and puffed until he had it going properly. The presence of the Gunsmith in town had given him an idea. Now all he had to do was wait for the man's arrival.

Maybe it was time to finally put things right in Marion and Orange counties.

THIRTEEN

When Clint entered the Ox Bow, it was almost filled to capacity. The gaming tables were going, and there were about four girls in gaily colored dresses working the floor. A piano player in the corner was pounding away with more enthusiasm than talent.

Clint approached the bar and Hagen hurried down to him.

"Randle around?"

"Yes, sir," Hagen said. "He's in his office for sure. You want a beer first?"

"I do if I can take it with me."

"Sure thing."

Hagen drew Clint a cold beer, then led him to the back office.

"Eddie's been waitin' for ya," he said, knocking on the door and opening it. "Eddie, this here's Clint Adams."

Randle stood up from behind his desk and came around with his hand out.

"Any friend of Harry Dial's is welcome in my

place," he said. "Newly, that beer and any other this man has are on the house."

"Okay."

"Now get outta here and get me one."

Hagen tossed his boss a jaunty salute and left.

"Have a seat, Mr. Adams."

"If we're both friends of Harry Dial's, I guess you should call me Clint."

"And I'm Eddie."

Hagen came back in with a mug of beer, handed it to Randle, and left.

"What's on your mind, Clint?"

"I guess you know about Harry's big game."

"I heard it was canceled," Randle said. "Wondered if you was one of the players when I heard you were in town lookin' for me."

"I was supposed to be," Clint said. "Rode a long way to play in that game."

"Wasted ride."

"Exactly. Harry suggested I come over here to see if you had anything for me that might make the trip less of a waste of time."

"Like what?"

"Like a game?"

"Ain't no big gamblers in town right now, Clint," Randle said. "Best I could do for you would be a nickel-and-dime game. That ain't worth your while."

"Not even close," Clint said. "I guess I better head back west then, get back on my own side of the Mississippi."

"Before you do that," Randle said, "let me bounce an idea off of you."

"What kind of an idea?"

"Somethin' else that might make the ride worth it for you."

"Like what?"

"Can I depend on you to keep this between you and me?" Randle asked.

"I don't know what I'm keeping between you and me," Clint said.

"I'll have to ask you to agree anyway."

"Well . . . since you're a friend of Harry's, I guess so," Clint said.

Randle opened a drawer, took something out, and tossed it on the desk. It landed with a tinny ring.

Clint leaned forward and found himself looking at a deputy marshal's badge.

"You offering me a job?" he asked.

"That's mine," Randle said. "It's federal."

"Oh." Clint sat back. "So I guess that means you're more than a saloon owner."

"Yes, sir," Randle said. "I was sent here four months ago to catch a gang that's been hitting banks, stages, and trains in Marion and Orange counties. This saloon owner thing is a cover."

"And in that four months, what have you come up with?" Clint asked.

"A theory."

"That's all?"

"Yep."

"You got any backup?"

"Nope."

"You send your boss your theory?"

"Yes."

"And?"

"No backup," Eddie Randle said. "I'm told that would take facts."

"So you're stuck here alone."

"That's about the size of it."

"What about your bartender?"

"He doesn't know anything."

"The local law?"

"Can't trust him."

The door opened. Clint reacted before Randle could. He took off his hat and tossed it on the desk so it covered the badge.

"Thought you'd need two more beers, gents," Hagen said, handing them out.

"Thanks, Newly," Randle said, "but knock next time, huh?"

"Oh, uh, sure, Eddie, sure," Hagen said, taking his leave.

"Thanks," Randle said, retrieving the badge from beneath the hat and putting it back in the desk.

Clint left his hat where it was, and pulled on the beer some.

"So what do you want from me, Eddie?"

"I thought you might wanna stick around, maybe help me out."

Clint narrowed his eyes. "Harry knows, doesn't he?"

"Yeah, but Harry's no man with a gun."

"And that's why he sent me here."

"That's my guess."

"He didn't send you a telegram telling you I was coming?"

"No telegraph office in Ajax," Randle said. "This setup is Harry's. I had nothin' to do with it."

"But you'll take advantage of it."

"Hell, yeah," Randle said. "I'd be a simpleton not to see the possibilities, and an idiot not to take advantage of them."

"I can't argue with you there."

"So whataya say?" Randle asked. "I can't offer you any compensation. I doubt I could get the government to go for that."

"No, I wouldn't expect it," Clint said.

"So?"

"You any good with an iron?"

"I get by," Randle said. "I can do my job."

Clint stuck a finger in his ear and wiggled it around while he thought.

"Let me give it some thought overnight," Clint said. "Tomorrow, if I agree, then you can tell me what your theory is."

"That's fair," Randle said. "I meant what I said, too. You drink free here."

Clint grinned and said, "And you said you couldn't offer any compensation."

FOURTEEN

Clint left Eddie Randle's office, wishing he had Harry Dial there to strangle at that moment.

He walked to the bar, and Newly Hagen had a beer waiting for him.

"Get your business with the boss done?" he asked.

"Maybe," Clint said.

"Sorry if I walked in at the wrong time," the bartender said.

"No problem."

"You ain't here lookin' for . . . somebody, are ya?" Hagen asked.

"Like who?" Clint asked.

"Jeez, I don't know," the bartender said.

"Have you done anything I should be looking for you for?"

"Me? No, no," Hagen said. "I was just wonderin'— I mean, your reputation and all . . ."

Clint stared at him.

"I didn't mean nothin'."

"Yeah, I know," Clint said. "I was just looking for a poker game, Newly."

"Poker game," Hagen said. "Lots of fellas here play poker."

"Yeah, but I was looking for a big game."

"You carryin' a lot of money?"

The bartender's raised voice caught the attention of others at the bar, who sized Clint up.

"No, Newly, I'm not carrying a lot of money," Clint said loudly. "Are you trying to get me killed?"

"Sorry."

Clint put his beer mug down on the bar, half finished, and said, "Good night, Newly."

As Clint walked away, Hagen whined, "Aw, I didn't mean nothin'."

Clint was sure the bartender never "meant nothin'" but he was too free with his mouth, and he didn't think before he spoke. All Clint needed was for somebody in town to think he was carrying a large sum of money.

Walking back to his hotel, he thought about Eddie Randle's request. Did he really want to get involved in something like this just because his poker game had been canceled? It seemed pretty obvious to him that Harry Dial had sent him here figuring his buddy Eddie Randle could use the help. He doubted that Dial's game had been a ruse from the beginning to get him here. That was giving Dial too much credit for being sneaky. He was a gambler, but he wasn't a sneak. He had probably sent Clint to Dexter thinking his two friends could benefit from each other.

Clint wondered if he'd be able to walk away from this now that he knew Randle was federal law and needed help. After all, anyone who knew him knew he couldn't just walk away from a lawman in trouble.

He was a sucker for somebody in trouble, especially a lawman.

After Clint left the office, Eddie Randle, whose real name was Deputy U.S. Marshal Eddie Reed, sat back in his chair, clipped a cigar, and puffed on it until he had it going properly.

Being undercover was not for him. These four months were the longest months of his life. This was definitely going to be his last undercover assignment. He couldn't wait to get back on a horse and back on the trail of men he knew were criminals. When he had taken this assignment, he hadn't thought it through properly. He wasn't a detective, he was a lawman. From the start he didn't know who his prey was, and even though he had a good idea now, he still couldn't prove it.

If he could secure the help of Clint Adams, maybe he could wrap this thing up—finally—and get back to wearing a star.

He took the badge out of the drawer again and held it in his hand. He'd been so proud the first time he'd pinned it on ten years earlier that he'd slept with it on the first night. He didn't even care that it pinpricked him awake three times.

He missed wearing it. He held it in his palm, closed his hand around it tightly, then returned it to the desk drawer.

With Clint Adams gone and Eddie Randle in his office, the bartender, Newly Hagen, crooked his finger at Sean Sanchez. Sanchez's mother had been an Irish whore and his father a Mexican bandito. The man hung around the saloon and would do anything for a dollar.

"What's up, Newly?"

Hagen handed him a silver dollar and said, "Go and find me Doyle."

FIFTEEN

When Clint woke the next morning, he knew what he was going to do. But first he was going to have breakfast and take a look around town. Maybe even drop in on the local law and see if he could figure out why Randle didn't trust him.

He went to the same café where he'd had the steak, and had some eggs and grits and biscuits. Over a second pot of black coffee that wasn't too bad, he realized he'd neglected to ask Randle if that was his real name. That meant that even if he wanted to, he couldn't check up on him. After all, he could've killed a deputy U.S. marshal and stolen the badge from him. But that was being a little too inventive with his thinking. If Randle was a phony, why ask Clint for help?

He paid his check and stepped outside the café, stopped there, and looked around. The town was waking up; doors to stores were opening and people were hitting the streets.

He'd passed the sheriff's office on the way the day

before, so he knew where it was. He turned left and started walking.

"Why didn't you tell me about this yesterday?" Thomas asked John as they opened the front door.

"It slipped my mind."

"It slipped your mind that somebody who knows what we do came to town?"

"We got really busy, Tom," John said. "Ain't that a good thing."

"Being busy is a good thing," Thomas replied. "Having Doyle here in town ain't."

"Relax. He ain't gonna say nothin' to nobody," John said. "He's just waitin to hear from us."

"Oh, he's gonna hear from us, all right," Thomas said. "We gotta get rid of him."

"You mean kill him?"

"You know a better way to get rid of him?"

"We could use him," John said.

"How? For what?"

"If we really are gonna hit two banks, it might be handy to have an extra gun."

"We're a family business, John," Thomas said. "What are you thinkin'?"

"You're the one who wasn't convinced about the kid," John said.

"I'm not."

"I tell you what," John said, "I'll ride with the kid and you ride with Mort. Whatever we do, you don't have to go with Sammy, okay?"

"Okay," Thomas said, "okay, I'm sorry. So what do we do about Doyle?"

"If we kill 'im, we're gonna bring attention to ourselves."

"Well," Thomas said, "I guess that depends on how he dies, don't it?"

Mort came out of the house and found Sam standing on the porch.

"What's wrong, kid?" he asked. "I thought you was seein' to the chickens."

"Why do we do this, Mort?"

"Do what?"

"Keep this farm goin'," Sam said. "And the store. Why bother with either one when most of our money comes from jobs?"

"Who says most of our money comes from jobs?" Mort asked. "That money is what we use to keep the store and the farm goin'."

"Yeah," Sam asked, "but why?"

"Because Pa started this farm, Sam," Mort said, "and Ma started the store. If we let either one die, then we let them die, too."

"But they *are* dead."

"You don't remember them so well because you was small when they died," Mort said. "It's easier for them to be dead for you than it is for me, or Tommy or Johnny."

Sam screwed up his face.

"Yeah, I know, kid," Mort said, "you don't understand. See? That's why it's real important that you just do what you're told."

"But Mort, I don't think—"

"Don't think, kid," Mort said. "Just do what I told you to do."

He took the boy by the shoulders, turned him around, and gave him a push, wondering if he was also going to have to give him a kick in the pants like his old man used to have to give him all the time.

SIXTEEN

Clint entered the sheriff's office, found the sights and smells of it very familiar. With police departments popping up in Western towns, he'd expected to find that here in Indiana. Instead, he found an Old West office, and a lawman seated behind the desk.

The sheriff looked to be in his forties, and looked up at Clint with unconcerned eyes.

"Good morning, Sheriff," Clint said.

"Morning," the man said. "What can I do for you, mister?"

"I'm just passing through your town, Sheriff," Clint said. "Thought I'd stop in and announce myself."

"Any particular reason you should be doin' that?" the lawman asked.

"My name is Clint Adams."

The sheriff stiffened for a moment, then said slowly, "Well, yeah, I guess that would be a pretty good reason. When did you get here?"

"Yesterday."

"Any particular reason?"

"Like I said," Clint replied, "I'm just passing through."

"Gonna stay awhile?"

"Seems like a nice little town," Clint said. "Might stay a few days."

"You ain't here lookin' for somebody, are you?" the sheriff asked.

"You're the second person to ask me that," Clint said.

There had been a shingle on the wall by the front door that said "Sheriff Lou Perry." "Sheriff Perry," Clint said, "I'm not here looking for anybody. In fact, I can honestly tell you that a couple of days ago I had no idea I'd even be here."

"Well," Perry said, "I guess you got every right to pass through a town."

"Thanks."

"Thank you for stoppin' in and lettin' me know."

"You can pass it on to your deputies, too," Clint said.

"Only got one deputy," the sheriff said, "but yeah, I'll let him know. Where are you stayin'?"

"The Hotel Dexter."

"You sure?" Perry asked. "We got two—"

"I know," Clint said. "Hotel Dexter and Dexter Hotel. I can see how somebody might get confused, but I'm sure."

He stood up, and the sheriff followed.

"Well," the lawman said, "thanks again."

"Been sheriff here long?" Clint asked.

"About a year," Perry said.

"Seems like a pretty quiet town to me."

"It has its moments," Perry said, "but we're pretty happy with it."

"I was over in Ajax a couple of days ago," Clint said, "heard there might've been some trouble in these two counties."

"Who'd you hear that from?"

Clint shrugged.

"In the saloon, I think," Clint said. "Might've been the bartender."

"Well, like I said, we have our share. Might've been a robbery or two hereabouts. But me and the sheriff over in Orange County have got it covered."

"Well, that's good to hear," Clint said, heading for the door. "I see you in the saloon, Sheriff, maybe I can buy you a drink."

"That'd be right nice of you, Mr. Adams," Perry said. "Thanks."

"Have a nice day."

Clint stepped outside. He felt sure the sheriff had been lying when he asked him about the trouble. Admitting to "a couple" of robberies meant there had been a lot more than that. The lawman's lies pretty much confirmed what Eddie Randle had told him.

There was trouble in these two counties.

After Clint Adams left the office, Sheriff Lou Perry vigorously dry washed his face with both hands. What was he supposed to do with somebody like the Gunsmith in town? And asking questions, to boot?

He stood up, strapped on his gun, and grabbed his hat. He figured the only thing to do was go see the mayor and let him make a decision. After all, that's what he'd wanted when he ran for office, and that's what the people paid him for.

SEVENTEEN

The front door of the Ox Bow was slightly ajar when Clint arrived. From inside he could hear the sound of a broom sweeping across the floor. He stepped in and left the door ajar.

"Good morning," he said.

Sean Sanchez looked up from his sweeping and stared at Clint.

"We ain't open," he said.

"That's okay," Clint said. "Eddie's expecting me."

"Hey," Sanchez said, pointing, "ain't you the Gunsmith?"

"That's right."

"Wow," the younger man said. He dropped his broom to the floor. "Can I shake your hand?"

"What's your name?"

"Sean Sanchez."

"That's an unusual name," Clint said. "Irish and Mexican?"

"Yes, sir."

"Interesting," Clint said. "Sure, we can shake hands."

The young man came toward him. Clint noticed that Sean Sanchez did not wear a gun. Before shaking hands, Sanchez wiped his on his pant leg, then clasped Clint's.

"Is Eddie around?" Clint asked, releasing Sanchez's hand.

"Yeah, he sure is," Sanchez said. "He's upstairs in his room, but he'll be down any minute. He usually comes down around this time."

Clint briefly considered going upstairs to Randle's room, but he remembered how he had found Harry Dial when he knocked on his door a few days ago.

"Okay," Clint said. "I'll wait. Is that coffee I smell?"

"Yeah, yeah, that's one of my jobs around here," Sanchez said. "I make the coffee in the morning, clean up. Someday Eddie's gonna make me a bartender."

"Well, that sounds good," Clint said.

"You want a cup?"

"I do, yeah," Clint said. "Thanks."

"Comin' right up," Sanchez said.

The chairs were all on top of the tables, so Sanchez took one down and said, "Have a seat."

"Thanks, Sean."

Clint sat down. Sanchez hurried behind the bar, poured a cup of coffee, and hurried back with it.

"You want some cream or sugar or somethin'?"

"Nope," Clint said, "just like this."

He tasted it. It was the best coffee he'd had since leaving Texas.

"Wow, that's just the way I like it."

"Strong," Sanchez said. "My pappy used to like it strong."

"Your pappy sounds like he was my kind of man."

"He was a drunk," Sanchez said, "and a bandit, but he was my pappy."

Clint didn't quite know what to say to that, but he was saved from having to come up with something. They both heard a door open and close upstairs, and then Eddie Randle came down the stairs.

"Hey, good mornin', Clint," Randle said.

"Mornin'."

Sanchez took another chair down for Randle, then hurried to the bar to get his boss a cup of coffee.

"Thanks, Sean."

"Sure thing, Eddie."

"I see your broom on the floor," Randle said. "You done sweepin'?"

"No, sir," Sanchez said. "I was just gettin' Mr. Adams some coffee."

"Well, you can finish up now, kid."

"Okay, Eddie. See ya, Mr. Adams."

"Clint, Sean," Clint said. "You can just call me Clint."

"Okay, Clint!"

He walked over, picked up his broom, and continued sweeping.

"He tells me you're going to make him a bartender."

"He can have the whole place if he wants it," Randle said. "I want to finish my assignment and get the hell out of here."

Clint lowered his voice and asked, "Undercover work not for you?"

"Not at all," Randle said. "I'd rather be in the saddle, tracking a killer across a mountain or desert, than this. And I ain't no damned detective either."

"Why'd you take the assignment then?"

"I thought I was lookin' for somethin' different," Randle said. "Well, I ain't gonna look for somethin' different no more."

"Sometimes it's best to stick to what we know best," Clint said.

Randle sipped his coffee and asked, "You got any good news for me this mornin'?"

"Well, I think I might, Eddie," Clint said.

Randle, looking excited, leaned forward and kept his voice low.

"You're gonna do it?"

"Maybe you should send Sean on an errand, Eddie," Clint suggested.

"Sean's okay, Clint. He ain't very smart, but he's okay."

"I think we ought to play this safe, Eddie," Clint said, "don't you?"

"Yeah, you're probably right. Hey, Sean!"

"Yeah, Eddie?"

Randle took some money out of his pocket and said, "Would you go over to Archer's General Store and get me some cigars?"

"Sure, Eddie, sure." Sean took the money. "Anythin' for you, Mr.— I mean, Clint?"

"No thanks, Sean."

"I'll be right back, Eddie."

"Take your time, Sean," Eddie Randle said, "take your time."

EIGHTEEN

"I'll make myself available to you," Clint told Eddie Randle, "but you've got to tell me everything. Don't keep anything back."

"Like what?" Randle asked. "What do you think I'd hold back?"

"I need to know what we're up against," Clint said. "One man, two, a gang? How big a gang?"

"It looks to me like a gang," Randle said, "three, maybe four of 'em."

"Okay," Clint said. "What've they done?"

"Everythin'," Randle said. "Before I got here, they'd hit stages, banks, and trains. They took a federal payroll off a train, and that's what got me sent here."

"And since you've been here?"

"They've kept hittin'," Randle said. "Two stagecoaches and a bank since I been here."

"Any witnesses?"

"Plenty, but the men have been masked."

"No names?"

"They've been careful not to call each other by name," Randle said.

"Sounds like a disciplined gang."

"I wish they weren't," Randle said. "They might be easier to catch."

"Okay," Clint said, "so tell me what you know, or what you think you know."

"What I think I know," Randle said, "is that—"

He was interrupted when the front door slammed open and three men entered. They staggered in, stopped, and looked around. They were all armed.

"Hey, is this place open?" one of them shouted.

"Wow, a saloon open this early?" another said. "What a great town."

"Sorry, fellas," Randle said, "we ain't open yet."

"But your door's open."

"We're just airin' the place out," Randle said. "Come back in a few hours."

The third man screwed up his face and said, "But we want some whiskey now."

"You fellas seem like you already found some whiskey this morning," Clint said.

"What you care, fella?" one of them asked. "What you doin' here anyway, if it's closed?"

Randle stood up. He was wearing a sidearm on his right hip.

"Time for you fellas to go," he said. "Come on. Out the door."

"Or what, friend?" one of them asked.

Clint stood up, stood next to Randle.

"You don't want to know the answer to that question, friend," Clint said.

The three men eyed Clint and Randle standing side by side, and then one of them said, "Aw hell, this place is a dump anyway. Come on, boys."

The three men backed out, and Randle locked the door behind them.

"What about Sean?"

"He'll knock," Randle said. "Hey, we make a good team."

"So far," Clint said. "You were getting ready to tell me something?"

"Yeah, I was."

Before he did, however, he retrieved the coffeepot from behind the bar and brought it to the table. He poured both their cups full and then sat down.

"You asked me what I thought I knew," Randle said. "We've got a family in town named Archer. Brothers, actually."

"You sent Sean to Archer's General Store," Clint said.

"Right," Randle said. "They also have a farm outside of town. There are four of them, and everyone in town thinks they're merchants and farmers."

"And what do you think?"

Randle sipped his coffee and said, "I think they're the gang."

NINETEEN

"Thomas and John run the general store," Randle said. "Mort runs the farm. He's the oldest."

"You said there were four."

"Sammy," Randle said. "He's the youngest. Might be eighteen."

"So four of them," Clint said. "Nobody else. Like parents?"

"Dead."

"Sisters. Other brothers?"

"Just them."

"And they're from here?"

"Born and bred, from what I know," Randle said. "Back from before this town was called Dexter. Maybe back from before there was even a town here."

"And what makes you think they've been pulling the robberies?"

"The farm's a failure," Randle said, "and I wouldn't exactly call the general store a success."

"Is there another store in town?"

"Peck's Mercantile," Randle said. "Most people shop there."

"So then why are they open?"

"Exactly."

"And you've been in there?"

"Yeah," Randle said, "I've been doin' my shoppin' in there."

There was a knock on the door at that time. Randle unlocked it and let Sean Sanchez in.

"Here ya go, Eddie," Sanchez said, "your cigars."

"Thanks, Sean," Randle said. Sanchez started forward, but Randle stopped him. "I won't need you for a while, Sean."

"But I gotta finish sweepin', Eddie."

"That's okay, Sean," Randle said. "I'll take care of it. You come back later, when we're open."

"Okay, Eddie."

Sean Sanchez backed out and Randle locked the door again.

"You make friends with any of them?" Clint asked.

"No," Randle said. "I mean, I'm acquainted with Tom and John because I've seen them at the store."

"Don't know Mort?"

"No."

"Or Sam?"

"No."

"Okay," Clint said. "How do you want to play this?"

"I figure they're gonna have to pull another job soon," Randle said. "Between us maybe we can keep an eye on them."

"How about if I go out to the farm and have a look around?" Clint said.

"What for?"

"Just to see what I can see. None of the brothers

have seen me, and even if they have, they don't know I'm working with you."

"Well, okay," Randle said, "go ahead. Maybe you'll find somethin' to link them to the jobs."

"Have you been out there at all?"

"No," Randle said. "Couldn't think of a reason to give 'em, and I didn't want to get caught snoopin' around."

"I'll take a look. How do I get there?"

Randle gave him directions.

"But what will you tell them if you get caught?" Randle asked.

"Maybe I'll tell them I'm looking to hook up with a well-run gang."

"It'd be better if you just didn't get caught."

"I'll do my best."

Clint headed for the door, unlocked it, opened it, then turned.

"By the way," he said, "what's your real name?"

"Reed," the man said, "Deputy Marshal Eddie Reed."

TWENTY

Clint decided not to waste any time. When he left the Ox Bow, he went directly to the livery to get his horse.

"I'll show you where he is," the liveryman said, "unless you want me to saddle him for you."

"Can you?" Clint asked.

"I can saddle a horse, mister," the man said.

"No, I mean . . . will he let you?"

"Sure," the man said. "We're gettin' along just fine."

"What's your name?"

"Beau."

"Okay, Beau," Clint said. "Go ahead and saddle him."

"Wanna watch?"

Clint was shocked at how docile Eclipse was while Beau saddled him. The man spoke to him the whole time, stroked his neck and withers—things the big Darley wouldn't allow anyone else to do, except Clint.

"Here ya go," Beau said, walking the horse to him and handing him the reins.

"Looks like you guys really are getting along," Clint commented.

"I know how to handle horses."

"Yes, you do," Clint said. "My apologies."

"No need," the man said. "You gonna bring him back here?"

"Yes," Clint said. "I'm just taking him out so he— and I—can stretch."

"Good," Beau said. "A horse like this deserves to be ridden."

Clint walked Eclipse outside before mounting up.

Clint gave Eclipse his head when they'd cleared the town limits. The big gelding ate up the ground, the breath exploding from his nostrils. After they'd run for a couple of miles, Clint took control and turned the horse in the direction of the Archer farm. Two more miles and he topped a rise and found himself looking down at the farm.

It was sad. The house was in disrepair, as was the barn. There were some chickens running around, but they were scrawny things. Any inference that this was a going concern was an obvious lie. He wondered about the intelligence of the Archer brothers. If they were robbing and expecting people to think their money came from their farm . . .

Now he realized he should have gone to see the general store before he came out here. But since he was here, he decided to try and get a closer look.

He found a likely place to hide Eclipse, a copse of trees that would keep the animal out of sight while he approached the farm on foot.

He came at it from behind the barn. No one would be able to see him from the house if they were looking out the window.

The barn had a back door, so he had no trouble getting in. Once inside, he found supplies, but not the kind of supplies one would need to run a farm. There were two horses, probably saddle horses, because the plow that was in there hadn't been in a field in a long time. Yep, there were two worn saddles inside the stalls with the horses.

Underneath a tarp he found an open wooden crate with rifles and handguns inside. An arsenal. In another box he found maps of both Orange and Marion counties. He also found an envelope with train schedules inside. And stagecoach schedules.

He was delving into another box when he heard someone at the front door. Hurriedly, he covered everything with the tarp, then looked for cover. His first instinct was to hide behind the tarp himself, but whoever was entering the barn night be coming to check on the contents.

He found cover behind the decrepit plow.

From there he watched as a young man removed the tarp and reached into the crate of weapons. With a big grin he took out a rifle, sighted down the barrel, and pretended to shoot something. He returned the rifle, then did the same routine with a handgun.

Another man entered, older but resembling the

first. Clint reckoned he was looking at Mort and Sam Archer.

"What are you doin', Sammy?" the older man asked.

"I, uh, I'm just lookin' at the guns."

Mort joined Sam and took the pistol from his hand.

"Pickin' one out for yerself?"

"I'm gonna need a gun, Mort."

"You're gonna have to learn to use one first, kid," Mort said.

"Will you teach me, Mort?"

"Tommy's the hand with a gun," Mort said. "That's why he hates bein' behind the counter at the store. But he's also the smartest of us, so he needs to run the store."

"He's smarter than you, Mort?" Sam asked. "You're the oldest."

"Bein' the oldest don't make you the smartest, kid," Mort said, putting the gun back in the crate. "Look, Tommy will pick a gun for you, Sammy. And give you a couple of quick lessons."

"Do you know what the next job is yet, Mort?" Sam asked.

"Not yet, Sammy," Mort said, "but we'll figure it out." He slapped the boy on the back. "Come on, let's go back into the house."

"Mort?" Sam asked as they walked to the door.

"Yeah, kid?"

"Are we ever gonna leave this farm?"

"This farm is home."

"Yeah, but . . . it's fallin' apart."

"That's because none of us are farmers, like the old man was. You wanna leave the farm, Sammy?"

"Well, sure . . . don't you?"

"Eventually," Mort said as they went out the door, "I guess."

TWENTY-ONE

Clint came out from behind the plow, hurried to the front door, and watched the two brothers enter the house. When he was sure they were inside, he went back to the crates and boxes, which the Archers had now left uncovered by the tarp. Staring down at the guns and maps, he knew this wasn't enough evidence for a deputy U.S. marshal to act on. In the absence of witnesses who could identify the robbers, they were going to have to catch them in the act.

The maps of the two counties as well as the stage and train schedules could be for jobs they'd already pulled. He was going to have to find out from Randle where they had already hit.

And banks. There was no research material here about banks.

Mort had told Sammy that their brother Thomas was the smart one. Clint had to get inside the general store to see what else he could find.

According to Mort and Sammy, they hadn't picked out their next job yet.

Maybe he could figure out some way to help them along.

Clint rode back to town and returned Eclipse to the loving arms of Beau at the livery. He headed for the Ox Bow, but on the way he saw Archer's General Store across the street.

He changed direction and crossed the street.

Mort remembered that they had left the tarp off the crates.

"Sammy, go and cover the guns," he told his younger brother. "And don't play with them."

"Aw, Mort . . ."

Sam left the house and went back to the barn. He covered the crates and boxes with the tarp, but as he turned to leave he noticed the back door to the barn was ajar. Nobody used that door—ever. It had always been closed tight.

He walked to the door, swung it open and closed a few times, then looked at the dirt beneath his feet. There were a man's boot prints there, and they looked fresh. He turned and looked down at the floor of the barn. Mort had been teaching him to track, mostly for hunting, and he had picked it up pretty quick.

These boot prints did not match any of his brothers' boots.

Somebody had been in the barn recently.

He ran from the barn to tell Mort.

Mort Archer entered the barn with Sam and said, "Just stand there."

He walked inside, to the crates, to the back door and back.

"Am I right, Mort?" Sam asked anxiously. "Am I right?"

"It looks to me like you're right, kid," Mort said. "Somebody was in here, and recently. Maybe even sometime today."

"What do we do?"

"Saddle the horses," Mort said, heading quickly for the door.

"What for?"

"And pick a gun out of the crate for yourself," Mort added. "We're gonna track the bastard."

TWENTY-TWO

As soon as Clint entered the store, he saw what Randle had told him was true. The shelves were not very well stocked, especially not for a business being counted on to support a family.

There was one man present, standing behind the counter, wearing a white apron. Clint glanced around for something to show interest in so he wouldn't look suspicious.

"Can I help you find somethin'?" the man asked.

Stuck for an answer, Clint said, "Not really. To tell you the truth I'm just . . . killing time. I'm new to town, so I was taking a look around. I saw your store and thought I'd drop in."

"That's fine," the man said. "Just sing out if you need help."

"Seems to me most of the people hereabouts do their shopping at that other store," Clint said.

"That so?"

"Well," Clint said, "I mean, I passed by and they were pretty busy."

"Well," the clerk said, "they're bigger, and newer.

Folks generally check out a new store, but they usually end up comin' back."

"I hope that's true, for your sake," Clint said. "Oh, I just assumed you were the owner?"

"I am," Thomas said. "That is, one of them. Me and my brothers own it."

Clint approached the counter and put his hand out. "My name's Clint."

"Thomas," the other man said, "Archer, like the store." He shook Clint's hand.

"Pleased to meet you," Clint said. The smart one, he thought.

At that point another man came out of the back.

"Oh, didn't know you had a customer."

"This is my brother John," Thomas said. "Johnny, this is Mr. Clint . . . I didn't catch your last name."

Clint hesitated, then decided he really didn't have any reason to lie.

"Adams," he said, "Clint Adams."

Both men stared at him.

"The Gunsmith?" John asked. "That Clint Adams?"

"The only one I know of," Clint said.

John looked at Thomas, but spoke to Clint.

"What's the Gunsmith doin' in Dexter?"

"Like I told your brother," Clint replied, "I'm just passin' through. Thought I'd rest a couple of days. Took a turn around town, saw your store . . ."

"Yeah," Thomas said, "yeah, that's what he said."

"So you're not a customer then?" John asked.

"That's right."

"Well," John said, "it was nice to meet you. Thomas, I need your help in the back for a minute."

"Sure, Johnny," Thomas said. "'Scuse me, Mr. Adams. Uh, feel free to keep lookin' around. Maybe you will see somethin' you want, or need."

"Thanks," Clint said. "Don't want to take up too much of your time unnecessarily. I'll be out of your hair in a minute."

"Tom!" John said from the doorway to the back room.

"I'm comin'," Thomas said.

While both brothers were in the back room, Clint had a quick look around. There was dust on a lot of the products and on some of the glass display cases. This place didn't do much business at all.

The family business was pretty much a match for the family farm.

TWENTY-THREE

Mort followed the man's tracks to a copse of trees behind the barn. He dismounted and walked around.

"Whataya see, Mort?" Sam asked from astride his horse.

"Get down off your horse, boy," Mort said. "Come over here."

Sam dismounted and walked over.

"Careful," Mort said. "Don't trample the sign. See there?" He pointed.

"Tracks, made by a horse."

"But look at the size of 'em," Mort said. "That's some horse."

"Sure looks like."

"Get mounted," Mort said. "These here tracks ain't gonna be hard to follow."

"We gonna follow them all the way?"

"We are," Mort said as they both mounted up. "But I'm pretty sure they're gonna lead us to Dexter."

"We can stop in and see the boys."

"Yeah," Mort said, "we'll do that."

• • •

In the back room John said to Thomas, "What's the Gunsmith doin' here?"

"Lookin' around, John."

"I mean here in town."

"Why shouldn't he be in town?" Thomas asked. "Says he's passin' through."

"Don't that seem like a coincidence to you?" John asked.

"Coincidence?"

"Him comin' to town just when we're plannin' our next job?" John asked, lowering his voice.

"What's one got to do with the other, Johnny?"

"I'm just thinkin'—"

"Clint Adams ain't a lawman, is he?"

"Well, no—"

"So why should we be worried?" Thomas asked. He slapped his brother one the shoulder. "Don't go lookin' for trouble where there ain't none, Johnny."

Clint left Archer's General Store and stopped just outside. Coming down the street was Sheriff Perry. He stopped when he saw Clint.

"Doin' a little shoppin', Mr. Adams?" the lawman asked.

"Window shopping's more like it, Sheriff," Clint said. "Just taking a look around town."

"We got a new store, you know. One of them big mercantiles."

"So I heard."

"Pretty much takin' most of the business away from these poor Archers."

"What do you know about the Archers, Sheriff?"

"They're good boys," Perry said. "Hardworkin'. Got this store and a farm outside of town."

"I see."

"What's your interest in the Archers?" Sheriff Perry asked, suddenly suspicious.

"No interest really," Clint said. "I just met two of them inside."

"Tom and John?"

"That's right."

"Yeah, they run the store, their older brother Mort runs the farm. They got a young'un, too—Sam—but I guess he must be about eighteen by now."

"Pretty much a man, then."

"I guess."

"Well," Clint said, "guess I'll just keep walking, taking a look at your nice, quiet town. Maybe buy you that drink, later?"

"Maybe," the sheriff said. "I got rounds, so . . ."

The sheriff moved off, perhaps now suspicious about why Clint was asking about the Archers. Clint figured he'd better go and talk to Randle and let him know what he'd found out.

TWENTY-FOUR

Mort and Sam followed the tracks all the way to Dexter, just as Mort had predicted. Once they reached town, though, the tracks pretty much got trampled by all the traffic.

"What do we do now?" Sam asked.

"We'll stop in and see the boys, tell 'em we're in town," Mort said. "Then we're gonna check barns and livery stables, see if we can't locate the horse that belongs to these tracks."

"What do we do once we find it?"

"Find out who owns it, and then ask him what he was doin' snoopin' around our farm."

"This gonna hold us up from doin' our job, Mort?" Sam asked.

"Well, we ain't even decided what the job's gonna be yet," Mort said, "but once we do, we ain't gonna let nothin' keep us from doin' it. Now, come on, we'll ride around behind the store so nobody sees us."

"Who we hidin' from, Mort?"

"Whoever it was snoopin' at the farm, boy," Mort said. "I don't want them to know we're in town."

"Okay, Mort."

They rode around to the back of the store, dismounted, tied the horses off, and entered through the back door, into the storeroom.

"What the hell are you guys doin' here?" John asked, surprised.

"We followed some tracks here," Sam said.

"Tracks? To the store?"

"Where's Tommy?" Mort asked.

"Out front."

"Get 'im."

"He might be busy."

"Don't be funny, Johnny."

John went out front and came back with Thomas.

"Somebody was out at the farm snoopin' around today," Mort said. "The kid found tracks in the barn."

"Good eye, kid," John said. Sam grinned.

"We followed a man's boot tracks to a place where he'd left his horse. The horse's tracks would fit a big animal. Sam and me are gonna check around town, see what we can find."

"You think a lawman was out there?" John asked.

"I don't know why a star packer would be lookin' around us," Mort said, "and I sure don't think Sheriff Perry's got the brains or the guts."

"Then who?" Thomas asked.

"You guys notice any strangers in town?" Mort asked. "Anybody new?"

"Well," John said, "Doyle's in town."

"Doyle. What's he want?"

"He wants in on our next job."

"I knew we never should've used him," Mort said. "What do I always say?"

"Only family," Sam offered.

"That's what I always say," Mort said. "We'll have to take care of Doyle, but I don't think he's workin' for the law. Anything else?"

"Clint Adams," Thomas said.

"What?"

"He was here."

"That's the Gunsmith, ain't it?" Sam asked, wide-eyed.

"That's right."

"What the hell is the Gunsmith doin' here?" Mort asked.

"I don't know, Mort," Thomas said. "He said he was passin' through. And he wasn't wearin' any badge."

"Well," Mort said, "what are we supposed to do now?"

"I think," Thomas said, "havin' the Gunsmith here might work for us."

"How's that?"

"As a diversion," Thomas said. "He can attract enough attention away from us so we can do what we gotta do."

"That could work," Mort said. "All we gotta do is figure out what we gotta do."

"If we're gonna hit two banks," Thomas said, "they've gotta be close together."

"Like?" John asked.

Thomas shrugged. "Ten, twenty miles apart."

"That'd make it . . . What two towns are that far apart?"

Thomas grinned. "Dexter and Hopewell."

"Dexter?" John said, shocked. "You wanna hit the bank in this town? Where we live?"

"Why not?" Thomas asked, looking at each of his brothers in turn. "Who'd ever suspect it? And who'd suspect us of doin' it?

TWENTY-FIVE

Clint was sitting in the Ox Bow, nursing a beer at a back table, when the woman walked in. The place was quiet, just a couple of guys at the bar and one other table with a man nursing a whiskey.

She was tall and wide-shouldered, and had a long stride on her as she walked to the bar. Two things impressed him. She had a mane of chestnut hair that just about shimmered. The other thing was the Peacemaker on her hip. Not a new gun, but he could see how well cared for it was.

She stopped at the bar, collected a beer from Newly Hagen, exchanged a few words, then turned and looked at Clint. Her gaze was both bold and assessing. Finally, she picked up the beer and started over to him. Hagen watched her go with admiration.

When she reached Clint's table, she pulled out a chair and asked, "Do you mind?"

"Not at all," he said. "You can have a seat, but I'm going to need a name."

"Hannie," the woman said. "Hannie Welch."

"Go ahead, sit down, Hannie."

She sat and stared at him.

"You're Clint Adams."

"That's right."

"I heard you were in town."

"Funny," Clint said, "I didn't hear a thing about you."

"I was talkin' to the sheriff and he told me you were here."

"When did you get here?"

"Just today."

"What brings you here?" Clint asked. "Or, more important, what brings you looking for me?"

"I'm looking for a man named Doyle."

"I don't know him," Clint said. "What did he do?"

"He and some friends of his killed my sister and her husband. Left a little girl—my niece—without a mother and father. And my sister was my only relative."

"I'm sorry," Clint said. "So you're looking for him and his partners?"

"No," she said, "I found them. Three of them. He's the last one. I thought maybe you might've seen him."

"Sorry," Clint said, "but I don't know anyone named Doyle."

She fingered her beer mug, then lifted it and drained half of it. She had trail dust on her clothes, but none on her gun.

"You got a room yet?"

"Yeah," she said, "Dexter Hotel—I think."

"I know," he said. "It's confusing."

Suddenly, she slumped and looked very tired. But it only lasted a moment, and then she squared her shoulders again.

"You need some sleep."

"You're right about that."

"So go get some."

"Not yet," she said. "Not until I find Doyle."

"What's your next move?"

"Street by street," she said, "door to door, bartender to bartender . . ."

"He'll hear that you're looking for him."

"I hope he does," she said. "I want him to know I'm comin'."

"He'll be waiting for you."

"I wish he would," she said, standing up. "It's more likely he'll start runnin', but at least that would flush him out."

She left half her beer and started away.

"You're not a bounty hunter, are you, Hannie?"

"Not hardly," she said. "Just somebody who's lost her whole family."

"Except for your niece."

"Yeah."

"How old is she?"

"Four."

"Doesn't she need her aunt?"

"I'm no good with kids," she said. "She's in good hands with a family I know."

She started away again.

"You said you found the other three men?"

"That's right."

"Where are they now?"

"Six feet under," she said, "if anyone bothered to bury them."

She turned and left.

Newly Hagen listened to the conversation between Clint Adams and the woman. He heard her name, and heard the name of the man she was hunting.

Doyle.

He grabbed a towel and walked over to Clint's table. He picked up the beer the woman had left and mopped up the spot.

"Wow, huh?" he said.

"Yeah," Clint said. "Impressive."

"What was her story?"

"Looking for a guy."

"Wouldn't think a girl like that would have to look, huh?"

"No, she's not really looking," Clint said, "she's hunting."

"Yeah, I noticed she wears that gun like she knows how to use it."

"Yeah."

"Who's she looking for?"

Clint hesitated, then said, "I don't know, but I think she'll know him when she sees him."

Hagen nodded and asked, "You want another one?"

"No," Clint said, "I'll just nurse this one. Thanks."

"Sure," Hagen said. "You change your mind, just let me know."

TWENTY-SIX

Clint went over to the sheriff's office, and found a young man with a deputy's star sitting behind the desk.

"Help ya?" the boy asked.

"I was looking for Sheriff Perry," Clint said.

"Who are you?"

"Clint Adams."

The deputy rocked back in his chair. "Whoa! He told me you was in town."

"Do you know where he is?"

"Out and about," the young man said. "Makin' his rounds."

"He does that a lot, huh?"

"That's his job."

"Okay," Clint said, heading for the door.

"Can I tell 'im what you wanted?"

Clint turned and looked back at the deputy.

"Just tell him I was here looking for him," he said. "That's all."

"Will do."

"Uh, you wouldn't know anything about a man named Doyle, would you?"

"Doyle?" the deputy said. "I heard that name."

"Where? When?"

"Today," the man said, "earlier today. Some girl wearin' a gun came in and asked the sheriff about a man named Doyle."

"And?"

"And he told her about you."

"Then what?"

"She left."

"And after she left, is that when he went out on rounds?"

"Yeah," the deputy said. "Funny thing, too."

"What?"

"She went out the front door," the deputy said, "and he went right out the back."

"Was he in a hurry?"

"Now that you mention it," the deputy said, "yeah, he seemed like he was in a big hurry."

"And he didn't specifically say where he was going?" Clint asked.

"Naw," the deputy said, "he just said he was goin' on rounds, and I was to stay here."

"Okay, Deputy . . ."

"Gibbons."

"Deputy Gibbons," Clint said. "Thanks."

"Hey," the deputy yelled as Clint went out the door, "what's goin' on?"

Clint came back in the Ox Bow and yelled, "Eddie in the back, Newly?"

"Yeah, but—"

Clint kept going, got to the back door, and opened

it. Randle looked up from his desk. He had a ledger book open in front of him.

"Busy?"

"Doin' the books," Randle said, closing it. "Gotta make this place look legit. What's on your mind?"

"You ever heard of a man named Doyle?"

"Doyle," Randle said. "That a first name or a last name?"

"I don't know," Clint said. "I just heard the name today."

"Doyle," Randle said, again. "I don't know it, but then I haven't seen any wanted posters in months. What about him?"

"I just heard the name today, too," Clint said. "There was a woman in here looking for him."

Clint explained about Hannie Welch, told the undercover marshal her story.

"So she's killed three men and is lookin' for the fourth," Randle said. "What's that got to with what we're doin'?"

"Nothing," Clint admitted. "Just coincidence, her being here looking for man while you're here."

"What's such a coincidence about that?" Randle asked. "This woman isn't good-lookin', is she?"

"Oh yeah," Clint said. "She is."

Randle opened his ledger book again.

"Maybe we should keep our mind on business, Clint," Randle advised.

"Close the book," Clint said.

Randle closed it.

"I went out to the Archer ranch, and I had a look around the Archer store."

"You tell them who you were?"

"Nobody saw me at the ranch," Clint said, "but yeah, I didn't see the harm in telling Thomas and John who I was."

"And what'd they do?"

"Not much. They were pretty nice, let me look around the store."

"What about the farm?"

"Now, that's interesting . . ." He told Randle what he had found in the barn.

"So they got an arsenal out there," Randle said. "Probably all the weapons they've used on their jobs."

"These jobs they pulled," Clint said, "have they killed anyone?"

"Not until the last one, last month," Randle said. "They'd injured a few people, but last month they killed a guard on a stagecoach."

"So they weren't wanted for murder until then?"

"Right."

"Listen," Clint said, "the younger brother, Sam? This will be his first job. So for now, you're looking for three men."

Randle sat back, looking relieved.

"At least this confirms my suspicions," he said. "It has been the Archers pulling all these jobs."

"Guess you're not so bad at this undercover job after all."

"Yeah, well," Randle said, "don't tell my boss."

TWENTY-SEVEN

Beau looked up as the two men—one older, one barely more than a boy—entered the livery. The older man seemed to be studying the ground. Beau knew he'd find nothing there. There'd been so many horses back and forth over it, and Beau never swept the tracks away. He liked having all those hoofprints there.

"Help ya?"

The older man looked at him.

"We're lookin' for a horse leaves a big imprint behind," he said.

"Anything else about it?" Beau asked. "Markings that make it stand out?"

"No," Mort said. "Just bigger than most."

"Saddle horse?"

"Yeah."

"Lemme think," Beau said. "Seems there was a fella here a few weeks ago—"

"Sooner than that," Mort said. "Last day or so."

"Hmm," Beau said, "well, there was a guy here with a big gelding a few days ago."

"Still here?"

"No."

"Mind if I take a look at your animals?"

"Yeah, I do."

"Why?"

"Because they're my responsibility," Beau said. "Only me and the man who owns 'em can touch 'em."

"I don't wanna touch 'em," the man said. "Just look at 'em."

"Sorry," Beau said, "if you don't got a horse in here, I can't let ya in."

"Hey, listen, mister—" the younger man said.

Beau thought the kid looked like he was going to go for his gun, so he grabbed the rifle he kept close by for occasions like this. He reached into an empty stall and came out with it pointed at the younger man.

"Hey, whoa," the older man said, holding his arms out in front of the kid. "Take it easy, both of you. No guns."

"Take the boy and go," Beau said. "You got no business here."

"Sure, sure," the older man said, "we're goin'."

He forcefully turned the boy around and pushed him out of the livery.

Beau put his rifle down after the two men left, and walked back to the stall Eclipse was in. The horse left hoofprints behind no other horse could fill.

"Wonder what's goin' on, boy," he said, stroking the Darley Arabian's big neck.

Eclipse nickered and shook his head, then nodded energetically.

"Yeah," Beau said, "I guess I better find your buddy and let him know."

• • •

"Why'd you do that?" Sam demanded. "Why'd you let him talk to us like that?"

"What the hell's the difference," Mort said. "We got no beef with him."

"Well, he wouldn't let us in," Sam said. "Whataya think that means?"

"Means one of two things."

"Like what?"

"He either takes his job serious."

"Or?"

"Or the horse we're lookin' for is in there."

TWENTY-EIGHT

Clint didn't know why he went asking questions about Doyle. It wasn't what he had agreed to stay in town to do. But he kept thinking about Hannie Welch, riding around the countryside looking for the men who killed her sister, and killing them.

He had stepped down and started to cross the street when he heard a woman shout, and a crowd formed. He hurried across to see what was happening.

"She just fell," a woman said breathlessly. "I guess she fainted."

Clint saw Hannie Welch lying on the platform. There were people standing around her, but no one was trying to help. They were just gawking.

"Let me through," Clint said, pushing his way in.

He crouched next to her, saw her eyes flutter open.

"Hannie?"

He helped her to a seated position.

"What happened?" she asked, holding her head.

"You fainted," Clint said. "When's the last time you ate?"

"I-I don't remember."

"Okay, then," Clint said. "Come on. Can you walk?"

"Of course I can walk."

He helped her to her feet.

"Okay, that's all," Clint yelled to the onlookers. "It's all over."

He steered her away from the people.

"Where are we going?"

"To get you something to eat," Clint said. "I know just the place."

Minutes later they were seated in the small café across from Clint's hotel. Clint ordered Hannie a full steak dinner, while he had a bowl of beef stew. When both came, Hannie closed her eyes and leaned back.

"What's wrong?" Clint asked.

"It's been so long since I ate that I don't think I could handle all this."

"Would you like to switch?"

She looked across the table at his beef stew. It was a small bowl and did not take up anywhere near the room the steak platter did.

"Okay."

Clint switched the plates and started cutting into the steak. Hannie spooned some beef stew into her mouth and chewed.

"It's good."

"Even if it isn't," he said, chewing on a piece of steak, "it'll keep you from fainting again."

"I guess."

"Hannie," Clint said, "forgive me for saying so, since we've only just met, but you have to take better care of yourself. What if you had fainted right when you found your man, Doyle. He would've killed you."

"I suppose you're right."

As he watched, she began to eat faster and faster, so he slowed down. By the time she'd finished the stew, he still had half a steak left, and they switched plates again. He poured himself some more coffee and watched her eat.

"What you need after this is some rest," Clint said. "And by that I mean some sleep."

"Can't sleep on a full stomach," she said, "but I know what you mean."

"You can look for Doyle tomorrow."

She stopped cutting and looked across the table at him.

"Do you know something?" she asked. "Have you been askin' questions?"

"Well, just a few, on your behalf."

"And?"

"No one knows Doyle," Clint said. "Nobody's ever heard of him—I don't think."

"What do you mean, you don't think?"

"Finish the rest of that and I'll tell you."

She went back to work on the steak and the potatoes.

"I talked to the deputy," he said. "Apparently, after you talked to the sheriff, he ran out of his office through the back door."

"Why would he do that?"

"My guess is to warn someone."

"Doyle!"

"Maybe."

She started to get up.

"Then I need to talk to the sheriff again."

Clint stood quickly, put his hands on her shoulders, and pushed her back down.

"Hey!"

"Relax," he said. "Finish eating. Let's talk about this before you go accusing the sheriff of something. After all, he is the law."

She glared at him, then relaxed and popped the last piece of steak into her mouth.

"Can I have a piece of pie?" she asked.

TWENTY-NINE

Over pie—peach for Clint, apple for Hannie—they talked about the sheriff.

"I can't see any other reason for him to act like that," Clint said, "so your Doyle must be here."

"So I just have to keep looking for him."

"But not today," Clint said. "Maybe I can find something out today, but you should rest for the remainder of the day."

Hannie thought it over, then said, "Okay, maybe you're right. Why are you doin' this, by the way? Why are you helpin' me?"

"I'm not sure," Clint said. "It seems to be why I'm in Dexter, to help people."

"Who else?"

"Never mind," Clint said. "Let's finish our pie and get you to your hotel room. Then I'll see what I can find out."

"Okay."

"I'm fine, really," she said, when they got to her hotel room door.

"I just wanted to make sure you got here," Clint said.

She unlocked the door and opened it.

"I can't help thinking I should help you—"

"Go in and lie down," he said. "I'll come back and let you know if I find out anything."

She leaned over and kissed his cheek. She was tall enough to do it without having to stand on her toes.

"Come back anyway," she said.

Beau locked the livery and then walked toward town. He was starving, and was thinking of nothing but having something to eat.

"Okay," Mort said, "he's gone."

He and Sam came out from alongside the stable. They'd been standing there waiting, figuring that Beau had to leave sometime.

"Now what?" Sam asked.

"Now we get inside," Mort said, "and take a look around."

Sam started for the front door.

"No, Sammy," Mort said, "back door, so nobody sees us."

"Okay."

They went to the smaller back door, which was fairly easy to force. Once inside, they started going stall to stall, looking at the horses.

"What are we lookin' for?" Sam asked, staring at the ground.

Mort was about to answer when he saw the big black horse.

"That," he said, pointing.

"Wow," Sam said.

Mort moved forward toward the horse, but as soon as he got within striking distance the animal kicked out. Mort narrowly avoided having his head kicked off.

"Is that it?" Sam asked.

"Look there," Mort said, pointing to the ground in the stall. "Look at that track."

"It's big."

"It's not only big," Mort said. "That's it."

"Okay," Sam said, "so whoever owns this horse was in our barn?"

"Yes."

"So all we gotta do is find the owner."

"Right."

"And how do we do that?"

"We're gonna have to talk to that liveryman again," Mort said, "but this time a little harder."

THIRTY

Clint was walking away from Hannie's hotel when he heard his name being called. He turned and saw Beau from the livery running across the street toward him.

"Hey, Adams."

"Hello, Beau. Is everything all right with my horse?" Clint asked.

"Well, that depends."

"On what?"

"There was a couple of men at my place looking for a big horse."

"A big horse?"

"One that would leave really big hoofprints behind?" Beau said.

Damn, Clint thought. Had someone tracked him from the Archer place?

"Two men?"

"One older, one real young." Then he looked puzzled. "But they sorta looked alike."

"Like brothers?" Clint asked.

"Hey, yeah," Beau said, "like brothers."

"Where are you going now, Beau?"

"I'm gonna get me somethin' to eat."

"Then back to work?"

"Well . . . thought I'd get me a few drinks before I went back."

"That's good," Clint said. "Stay where there are people."

"Huh?"

"Just don't go back to the livery today," Clint said, "at all."

"I got to bed the stock down."

"Okay, then wait for me," Clint said. "Don't go back without me. Okay?"

"Well, okay."

"Meet me at the Ox Bow, and stay there until I come. Got it?"

"I don't understand it," Beau said, "but I got it."

"Good enough," Clint said. "Go ahead and get yourself something to eat."

"On my way."

As Beau walked away, Clint realized he was biting off more than he could chew now. First he was helping the deputy marshal, and now he was helping Hannie Welch. But he couldn't very well search for Doyle while the Archers were searching for him.

Except that even if they did find Eclipse, and even if they did realize that the big Darley was the one who had left the tracks behind, they still didn't know who owned the horse.

He decided to go to the livery and check on Eclipse.

• • •

"We can't kill Doyle," Thomas Archer said.

"Why not?" John asked.

They were in the back room of the store, which had been closed for several hours.

"If we kill him in town, it's gonna bring heat down on us," Thomas said. "And if we're plannin' on hittin' this bank, we don't need any heat."

"Ah, I still don't know about hittin' this bank," John said. "In our own town?"

"I told you, Johnny," Thomas said. "Nobody's gonna suspect us in our own town—as long as we don't kill Doyle here."

"So are you sayin' we don't kill Doyle," John asked, "or we don't kill him here, in town?"

"It'd be better if we could just get him to leave town on his own, so we don't have to kill him," Thomas said. "But yeah, if we can't get him to leave, we'll have to take him out somewhere and kill him."

"There's just one thing, Tom."

"What?"

"I'm no killer."

"John," Thomas said, putting his hand on his brother's shoulder, "we killed a man on our last job."

"That wasn't me," John said. "You and Mort did that."

"Yeah, and if we hadn't done it, you'd be dead," Thomas said. "That guy had a bead on you, brother."

"I know that!" John said. "I-I just don't know if I can kill Doyle in cold blood, you know?"

"Don't worry." Thomas patted his brother now.

"Don't worry. You won't have to. Mort or me, we'll take care of it. Okay?"

"Yeah, okay."

Suddenly, the back door opened. Mort and Sam came rushing in.

"We found the horse!" Sam said excitedly.

"Where?" Thomas asked.

"In a livery at the south end of town," Mort said.

"That's the one run by Beau Morgan," John said.

"Yeah," Mort said, "we met him."

"He pulled a gun on us," Sam said.

"Jesus," John said, "you didn't kill him, did you?"

"No," Mort said. "Little brother here wanted to use his gun, but I stopped him."

"Sammy," Thomas said, "you don't even know how to use that."

"You're supposed to teach me, Tom!"

"I know that," Thomas said, "and I will. Just don't touch that damn thing until I do. You'll get yourself killed."

"Aw, Tommy—"

"Shut up, Sam," Thomas said. "Mort, whose horse is it?"

"That we don't know," Mort said, "but we can find out tomorrow, or even tonight, from your friend Beau."

"I tell you what," Thomas said. "Why don't you leave that to me. Or rather, John, here." He squeezed his brother's shoulder. "He's been known to have a drink or two with ol' Beau."

"Yeah, at the Ox Bow," John said.

"Why don't you see if you can find ol' Beau and buy him a drink, John?" Thomas said. "I'll talk to

Mort and Sam about what we were just talkin'
about."

"What's that?" Mort asked.

"Doyle," Thomas said, "we were talkin' about
Doyle."

THIRTY-ONE

When Clint got to the livery, he found the front door locked tight. He went around to the back, and found that that door had been forced. He entered without drawing his gun. He had a feeling whoever had forced the door had been and gone.

He found Eclipse standing quietly in his stall.

"How you doin', big boy?" he asked. He ran his hands over the horse, checking for any damage. He was relieved to find none.

He looked at the other horses while he was there, and found nothing unusual. He left by the back door, figuring he'd return later with Beau.

He headed back toward the center of town.

When John Archer entered the Ox Bow, he didn't see Beau anywhere. It was about the time of day that Beau had a meal, so he decided to have a beer and wait for him.

"How you doin', John?" Newly Hagen asked.

"Okay, Newly," John said. "I'll have a beer."

"Comin' up."

When Newly returned with the beer, John asked, "Has Beau been in yet?"

"Beau? From the livery? No, not tonight. Should be in soon, though. He likes to have a few before he puts the stock to bed."

"Yeah, okay."

Hagen wiped a spot on the bar and then moved away. John hung his head over his beer, deep in thought. There was a lot of activity going on around him, but he didn't notice.

He was thinking about killing Doyle.

Eddie Randle—Deputy U.S. Marshal Eddie Reed— came out of his office to take a look at the house. The bar seemed full, and it looked like a good night as he walked around. He was about to go back to his office when he saw John Archer hunched over a beer at the bar. It had been a while since any of the Archers had been in his place. He decided to check it out.

He moved up alongside John, who didn't notice him. For someone who made his money robbing others, the man was a little too easy to sneak up on.

"Hey, John."

Archer started, turned his head.

"Oh, hi, Eddie," John said. "How're ya doin'?"

"Why so glum?" Eddie asked.

"Huh? Oh, I ain't glum," John said. "I'm just . . . thinkin'."

"About what? A woman? Girl trouble?"

"Naw, nothin' like that," John said. "Just . . . brother problems, ya know? Sometimes they get on my nerves."

"I wouldn't know about that," Randle said. "I got no brothers. No sisters either."

"Sometimes I wish I didn't have any brothers either," John said.

"Well," Randle said, "I'll leave you to finish your beer. Hey, Newly?"

"Yeah, Boss?"

"Give John one on the house when he's finished."

"Sure thing, Boss."

"Thanks, Eddie," John said.

"Don't mention it."

Randle left John at the bar and went back to his office.

Clint thought it was odd that he couldn't locate Sheriff Perry. He'd gone to the office and found it locked. He couldn't even find the deputy. The law was keeping a very low profile.

After about an hour he decided to go to the Ox Bow to get Beau.

As Beau entered the saloon, John turned and spotted him. When Beau saw John, it came to him who the two men at the livery had to have been. He knew John from the saloon, and he knew his brother Tom from the general store. He knew they had two other brothers, but he rarely—if ever—saw them.

The men at the livery had to have been Mort and Sam Archer.

John waved him over and said, "Buy you a beer?"

"Sure," Beau said, "why not?"

• • •

When Clint came into the Ox Bow, he saw Beau standing at the bar with John Archer. Neither of the men saw him, so he kept going, all the way to the back, to Eddie Randle's office door. He knocked and entered.

"You see John Archer out there?" Randle asked.

"Yes," Clint said, "I see he's having a beer with Beau, from the livery."

"Oh, Beau wasn't there when I saw him."

Clint sat down. "You have a conversation with John?"

"Just a short one, about brothers. He says sometimes they get on his nerves."

"Well, Mort and Sam tracked my horse to Beau's livery," Clint said. "He wouldn't let them see him, but I think they broke in and took a look."

"Even if they found your horse, they don't know who it belongs to."

"Not yet."

"So what are you gonna do?"

"I think it's a question of what we're gonna do," Clint said, "and then what they're gonna do."

"And do you have an answer to any of those questions?" Randle asked.

"Actually," Clint said, "I think I'm getting an idea."

"About what?"

"About a way to get them to hit when and where we want them to."

Randle sat back, laced his fingers behind his head, and said, "This I wanna hear."

THIRTY-TWO

Randle listened to Clint's idea, nodding as he did, and never interrupting.

"So let me get this straight," he said, when Clint was done. "You want the Archers to think that a lot of money is comin' in to the Dexter bank—"

"A *lot* of money," Clint said.

"Right, a *lot* of money, enough so they'll think that this could be their big score."

"Their last score," Clint said. "Every gang I ever dealt with was looking for that one big, last score."

"And then when they do hit the bank, we're waitin' for them."

"Right."

"And how would we get them to think that?"

"You have to get somebody to send a telegram to the bank, telling them about it," Clint said. "Or we have to get somebody at the bank to plant the lie."

"Like the bank manager?"

"Exactly like that."

"That'd be Walter Morris," Randle said. "I'd have to tell him who I really am."

"Yes."

"That'd be breaking my cover."

"Yep."

"And what about the local law?" Randle asked. "Perry? I don't trust him."

"I don't trust him either."

"Why not?"

Clint told Randle about Hannie Walsh and the man named Doyle, and the sheriff's reaction to the name.

"Why you gettin' involved in that?"

"Look, the girl needs help," Clint said. "She fainted in the street and I helped her, bought her something to eat. Then she told me about her meeting with the sheriff. It's enough to make me not trust him, so no, we'd keep him in the dark. In fact, let him think the same thing as the Archers."

"And the deputy?"

"Same thing," Clint said. "The fewer people who know what we're doing, the better."

"So you, me, and the bank manager."

"That's it."

Randle finally unlaced his fingers and sat forward.

"That could work."

"Okay then," Clint said. "First thing, you'll have to have a talk with the bank manager."

"Come with me," Randle said. "If we're all in on it, we should know each other."

"Okay," Clint said, standing up.

"What are you gonna do now?"

"I'm going to walk Beau back to the livery. I want to make sure he doesn't get killed."

"Okay," Randle said. "I'll meet you here in the morning."

"Right."

Clint left the office and headed for the bar to break up the conversation between Beau and John Archer.

"So how's business?" John asked Beau.

"Good," Beau said.

"Many strangers comin' into town?"

"Some."

"Lately?"

"A few."

Beau was being crafty. He thought John Archer was trying to get him to talk about Clint Adams's horse, for his brothers.

"Hey," he said. "how come I never see your other two brothers in town?"

"Oh, uh, Mort and Sam, they work pretty hard at the farm."

"Uh-huh. Never come into town to blow off steam?"

"No," John said, "they, uh, do that out there."

"Huh."

Beau saw Clint coming his way.

"Hey, Beau," Clint said.

"Mr. Adams."

"Ready?"

"Yeah."

John looked at Clint.

"Adams."

"Mr. Archer. Nice to see you again."

"Uh, yeah, likewise."

"I gotta bed down the stock," Beau said to John. "Thanks for the drink."

"Sure, Beau."

Outside, Clint asked, "What was that all about?"

"We have a beer together once in a while," Beau said, "but tonight he was trying to get information out of me, only he don't think I'm smart enough to know it."

"Information?"

"He was asking how business was, if there was a lot of strangers in town."

"I get it. And you were supposed to tell him about this man who rode in on a big black horse."

"Only I didn't," Beau said. "I asked him how come his other two brothers never come to town."

"You figured that out, huh?"

"Yeah," Beau said, "them two was his brothers. You don't have to hold my hand, ya know. I got a rifle at the livery. I can bed down the stock."

"I don't think they'd kill you, Beau," Clint said. "Not for this, but they might try to make you talk."

"Let 'em try."

"Wait a minute," Clint said, grabbing his arm. "Okay, I'll let you go back to work alone, but if they come back and want you to talk? Go ahead."

"What?"

"Tell them I own the horse. It's okay."

"Really?"

"Yeah, really. I want them to know."

Beau shrugged and said, "Okay, if that's what ya want."

"That's what I want. Thanks, Beau."

"Sure thing."

As he started away, Clint said, "Hey, wait."

"What?"

"Those questions John asked you?"

"Yeah?"

"Are there a lot of strangers in town?"

"Not a lot," Beau said. "You and one other man."

"A man named Doyle?"

"I don't know his name, but he was looking for a boardinghouse."

"Not a hotel?"

"Nope," Beau said. "He asked me about a boarding-house."

"And what did you tell him?"

"We got a few in town."

"And did you send him to one in particular?" Clint asked.

"I, uh . . ."

"I don't care if you're getting a kickback, Beau," Clint assured him.

"Well . . . yeah," he said, "I sent him over to Mrs. Buchanan's."

THIRTY-THREE

Clint considered going over to Mrs. Buchanan's and confronting Doyle, but that wasn't his decision to make. He didn't, however, want to tell Hannie where Doyle was tonight. She was probably still weak, still in need of rest. Beau told him that Doyle's horse was still at the livery, so there was little or no danger that the man had left town.

He decided to go to Hannie's hotel to check on her, but not tell her what he had found out.

He knocked on her door and waited. When it opened, she stared out at him a bit blearily.

"Hey," she said.

"Damn it, I woke you," he said. "And here I'm the one telling you to get some rest."

"It's okay," she said, rubbing her beautiful face. "Come on in."

Clint entered and closed the door. Hannie stood in the center of the room. She was wearing her trousers—men's trousers—and a loose-fitting shirt. No boots, her feet were bare.

"Did you find out anything?"

He didn't want to lie to her, and he had already hesitated too long, so he decided to go ahead and tell her the truth.

"I think your man, Doyle, is staying at a Mrs. Buchanan's boardinghouse in town."

She seemed to come awake right away.

"Okay, then, let's go."

"I don't think that's a good idea," he said, grabbing her by the shoulders as she tried to dart by him to the door.

"Why not?"

"Well, for one thing your gun belt's on the bedpost, and your feet are bare."

She looked down at her feet, then looked chagrined.

"Oh."

"You see?" Clint said. "You need to rest tonight and go after him in the morning, refreshed."

She touched her forehead, then sat down on the edge of the bed.

"You're probably right."

"I know I'm right," he said. "You want to be at your best when you face him."

She nodded.

"Okay," she said. "I'll sleep tonight and face him first thing in the morning."

"I can go with you, if you like," Clint said, then remembered he had an appointment in the morning. "No, wait . . ."

"That's okay," she said. "I've taken care of the others alone, I can do this."

"I'm sure you can," Clint said. "I'd like to help, though. I just have an appointment in the morning at the bank . . ."

"I don't want to interfere with your plans, or your life," she said.

"Believe me," Clint said, "my life is not here. I'm just here helping a friend."

"Someone else like me?"

"Not like you," he said. "He's a lot uglier than you are."

She covered her face and said, "I'm a mess."

"You look great."

"You think so?" she asked. "I've been in the saddle so long. I need a bath, my hair's a mess—"

She got up and walked to the mirror, stared at herself.

Clint walked over and stood behind her, slightly to the right. She was too tall for him to see over her head. He put his hands on her shoulders.

"Hannie, you know you're a beautiful woman."

"I might have been—once," she said. "Before all this ugliness. Before my sister was killed, before I killed three men . . ."

"You think killing three men changes who you are?" he asked.

"Doesn't it?" she asked. "How many men have you killed over the years? Dozens? How has it changed you?"

"You can't let it change you," he said. "You have to hold on to who you are."

She hugged herself and asked, "What if you don't know who that is?"

"Then you figure it out."

"I don't have time."

"You will, after tomorrow," he said. "Is Doyle the last one?"

"Yes."

"Then that's it," Clint said. "After tomorrow you can go back to who you were before this all happened. I mean, deep down, who you really are."

"I was a woman," she said, "but I don't feel like a woman anymore." Then he saw something come over her face. She turned to face him, his hands still on her shoulders.

"Can you make me feel like a woman again, Clint?" she asked.

"Maybe, Hannie," he said, "when this is all over . . ."

"No, no," she said, "now, I mean now." She undid one button on her shirt, then grabbed his hand and slid it inside. He felt the roundness of her breast, the hardness of her nipple against his skin . . .

"Make me feel like a woman," she whispered, turning his hand so that her breast rested in his palm.

"Hannie," he said in a thick voice, "do you really think this is a good idea?"

She opened more buttons on her shirt and it fell open. Her breasts were full and round, heavy. He found them cupped in his hands, as if his hands had a mind of their own. He flicked the nipples with his thumbs and she moaned.

"I don't care about anything else now," she said,

dropping her shirt to the floor. She slid her arms around his neck and pulled his head down. "Just this."

They kissed.

THIRTY-FOUR

She may have needed a bath, but to him her skin was smooth and sweet. He stripped her naked, stopping to kiss every inch of her. If she wanted him to make her feel like a woman, he was determined to do a good job of it.

When she was naked, he took her into his arms and kissed her, long and deep. She moaned into his mouth, reached for him, and started tugging at his clothes.

"God," she said against his mouth, "it's been so long."

Together they worked on his clothes until finally he was naked and his erection was prodding the air, demanding attention, which she was only too happy to offer.

She got on her knees and cooed at him while she embraced him, cupped him, stroked him. Finally he lifted her to her feet and walked her to the bed. The blanket was already pulled down, and they fell onto the sheets together.

"Oh God," she said as his hands roamed over her,

stroking and poking and prodding. He pressed his fingers into her, found her hot and wet.

"Oh!" she said, and this time it was like she'd been shocked by lightning. But then he kept stroking and she settled into it. She moved her hips in unison with his strokes and began to enjoy the waves of pleasure that were flowing over her.

"Don't ever stop that," she said.

"I have to stop," he told her, "so it can get better."

She smiled, stroked his face, and said, "I've never felt any better than this."

He put his mouth to her ear and whispered, "Just wait . . ."

Beau got back to the livery and unlocked the front door. He went in and began to see to the stock. It was no surprise to him when Mort and Sam Archer appeared in the doorway. This time Mort already had his gun out.

"One question, liveryman," Mort said, "and then we're on our way and you can keep on doin' what you're doin'."

Beau eyed the gun in the man's hand and asked, "Do I have a choice?"

"No," Mort said.

Beau waved his hand and said, "Then ask . . ."

Clint lifted his head from between Hannie's legs and looked up at her.

"Woo-wee!" she said, smiling down at him. "Do that some more!"

"You've had sex before, haven't you?" he asked. "I mean—"

"I'm thirty years old," she said, "and most of the

sex I've had has taken five minutes. I've never been with a man who could do all of . . . this."

"You've never had a man take his time with you?" he asked. He ran his hands up her body until he was covering her breasts. "No man should ever rush with a body like this."

She giggled like a schoolgirl.

"Oh my," she said, "I never had a man . . . talk like that."

He crawled up until he was lying on top of her. His rigid penis was trapped between them. To her it felt like a white-hot column of flesh.

"Hold your breath," he told her.

"What?"

"Just hold it."

She did.

He moved his hips, poked, slipped into her very slowly. If she hadn't been holding her breath, she would have gasped. He went slowly, sliding into her inch by inch until he was fully there.

"Oh my . . . ," she gasped, letting her breath out.

Thomas and John Archer lived above the general store. There was a kitchen, a sitting room, and each had his own bedroom. When the knock came at the door, John got up from the kitchen table and let his brothers Mort and Sam in.

"We found out who the horse belongs to!" Sam announced excitedly.

"Sit down, relax," Thomas said. "Have some stew, and tell us."

"You won't believe—" Sam started, but Mort silenced him with a look.

"Sit down, Sammy!"

Sam sat and John put a bowl of stew in front of him. It was a recipe their mother had left behind, and all the brothers knew how to prepare it, except Sam.

"So?" Thomas asked when they were all seated.

"The horse belongs to Clint Adams."

"Shit," Thomas said.

"I saw him talkin' to Beau in the saloon right after me," John said.

"Do you see what he did?" Thomas asked.

"What?" Sam asked.

"He told Beau to let us know."

"Why would he do that?" Mort asked.

"I don't know," Thomas said. "We don't know why he's here, but Beau probably told him you were looking for his horse."

"And what was he doin' out at the farm?" Mort asked.

"We don't know that either," Thomas said, "but we gotta find out."

"How?" John asked.

"Somehow," Thomas said, "and we gotta do it before we do anythin' else."

"I'm with John," Mort said. "How are we supposed to do that?"

"Well," Thomas said, "there's one obvious way to do it."

"What's that?" Sam asked.

"We can ask him."

THIRTY-FIVE

They rolled over, still connected, so that Hannie was on top. Her full breasts dangled in his face, so he had no choice but to bite them. She was sweating, and the smell was exciting him even more.

She rode him hard, grunting each time she came down on him, and soon her eyes were closed and her movements became mindless. He knew she no longer even knew it was him beneath her, she was just bouncing up and down, faster, faster, biting her lip, chasing the orgasm that was just ahead of her, like a carrot on a stick.

He gripped her hips, slid his hands up her strong, bare back, then pulled her down on him and cupped her buttocks, pulling her to him, trying to move even deeper into her. They writhed against each other, and before long he could feel her body trembling, before going taut as a bowstring. Then the arrow was loosed and she was crying out, grinding herself against him until he exploded inside of her with a loud cry of his own . . .

• • •

"Can you stay all night?" she asked.

She was lying in the crook of his arm, stroking his thigh with her fingertips.

"I don't see why not," he said. "If I leave, you'll probably head right for the boardinghouse and draw Doyle out of bed."

"We only just met and you know me that well?" she asked.

"We only just met and we're naked in bed together?" he asked.

She stretched and said, "I really needed this."

"I figured."

She pouted and asked, "Was it so hard on you?"

"If it hadn't been hard, we never would have got to this point."

"You're funny."

She moved her fingertips from his thigh to his penis. It flinched, then began to extend.

"Oh my," she said. "Again, so soon?"

"Why do most women say that?" he asked. "Is it such a surprise that I'm a man and I react when a beautiful woman touches me?"

"I don't know," she said, "let's see."

"What are you doin' here?" Sheriff Perry demanded.

"Take it easy," Doyle said. "Nobody saw me." He closed the back door behind him. He walked to the coffeepot and poured himself a cup.

"So when do you think this woman is gonna come after me?" he asked.

"I don't know," Perry said with a shrug, "maybe in the mornin'."

"I'll be ready."

"Just do me a favor," the lawman said. "Don't get yourself killed. I can't very well take off the Archers by myself."

"Yeah, about that," Doyle said, "you got anybody else to help us?"

"Don't worry," Perry said. "I'll have a few men. But you're the way in. You ain't heard from John yet?"

"No, not yet," Doyle said.

"Well, maybe you oughtta get back to the boardinghouse and stay there."

"Yeah, okay." Doyle put the coffee cup down. "I just wanted to stretch my legs."

He went to the back door.

"And when you kill this woman," Perry reminded him, "make sure it looks like self-defense."

"Don't worry," Doyle said, "just do your part, and I'll do mine."

"I could use a drink," Hannie said. "Do you want a drink?"

"What do you have?"

She got out of bed. He watched her pad naked to her saddlebags and retrieve a pint of whiskey, then pad back to the bed with it.

"Here ya go."

Clint took a pull from the bottle, then passed it back to Hannie. He watched her long throat work as she swallowed.

"Ah," she said.

"You want to get some rest now?" he asked.

She stared at him.

"Do you?"
"I think you need it."
"Do you need it?"
He laughed.

THIRTY-SIX

In the morning Clint met Eddie Randle at the Ox Bow, and together they walked to the bank. Randle had his business account there, so they were taken right in to see the bank manager. Once the door was closed behind them, Randle took out his badge.

"Mr. Morris," he said, "my real name is Deputy U.S. Marshal Eddie Reed."

"What?"

"This is Clint Adams."

"W-what?" Morris looked totally confused.

"We need to talk to you."

"About what?"

"A bank robbery."

Morris, normally red in the face, grew even redder. His mane of hair was as white as snow. He ran one hand through it.

"Bank robbery?" he repeated. "W-what bank is being robbed?"

"Well," Clint said, "if our plan works, yours."

• • •

Hannie Welch had watched Clint Adams dress and waited for him to go, then got out of bed herself, washed with the pitcher and basin, and quickly got dressed. She strapped on her gun, took a deep breath, and then went out to find Mrs. Buchanan's boarding-house.

Walter Morris finally calmed down long enough to sit and listen to the plan.

"And this would just be known to us?" he asked. "The three people in this room?"

"Deputy Reed is literally putting his life in your hands, Mr. Morris."

"And you say it's the Archer boys who have been pulling these robberies?"

"No question," Clint said.

"That's shocking," Morris said. "Those boys seem like nice fellas."

"Do they have an account here, Mr. Morris?" Randle asked.

"All their accounts are here."

"And can you tell us what their balances are like?" Clint asked.

"Well . . . that is confidential information."

Randle leaned forward and put his badge on the bank manager's desk.

"Ah, yes," Morris said, "of course. Let me get that information."

Doyle rose and came downstairs for breakfast. Mrs. Buchanan was an annoying old battle-ax, but she put out a breakfast he didn't want to miss. He wore his gun to the table, which got him a hard stare from the old woman, but he didn't care. If that other woman showed up for him during breakfast, he intended to be ready.

Morris came back in and sat down. He put some paperwork on the desk that he didn't show to either man.

"The figures are not good."

"So," Randle said, "unless they have some cash hidden away, they need to pull a job soon."

"You know, I've seen that farm and the store," Clint said. "I don't think they'll be able to resist a big score."

"So let me get this straight," Walter Morris said. "I just have to pretend we're getting a big deposit, right?"

"Right," Randle said.

"And we won't actually get robbed?"

"No," Randle said, "we'll be here waiting for them."

"When do you want me to let this information out?" the manager asked.

"As soon as possible," Randle said.

"Today," Clint added.

"Will you do it?" Randle asked.

Morris leaned forward and squinted at the badge that was still on his desk.

"Can you get me anything in print—"

"I can't send any telegrams, sir," the deputy said. "That would give me away."

"Of course, of course," Morris said.

"Sir," Clint said, "we won't let anything happen to your bank."

"We promise," Randle said.

"Well," Morris said, "very well."

THIRTY-SEVEN

Clint and Randle stopped just outside the bank.

"Okay," the deputy said, "the word goes out today, the Archers hear it, they decide to hit the bank . . . when?"

"They'll figure to hit the day the shipment comes in," Clint said. "That'll be the end of the week. We'll have to arrange for a stage to come in."

"What if they hit the stage?"

Clint rubbed his jaw.

"They probably will hit the stage," Clint said.

"Maybe," Randle said. "So we're gonna have to cover the stage and the bank."

"I suppose so."

"This is gettin' more complicated already."

"What's the closest town with a telegraph office?" Clint asked.

"There ain't one," Randle said, "since this town has one, this is where people come to send telegrams."

"If we could send one and have an empty, guarded armored wagon come to town, then they'd have to wait for the shipment to be moved to the bank."

"We can't do that," Randle said.

"Okay," Clint said. "What if we pass the word that the money is already in the bank?"

"Then folks would wonder when it came in."

"And they'd figure it came in at night, when everybody was asleep."

"You think?" Randle asked. "They won't suspect somethin's wrong?"

"I think the number we're putting out there is going to be too big to pass up, Eddie," Clint said. "Why don't you go back in and tell Morris what else to say?"

"And what're you gonna do?"

"I've got something else to take care of."

"The woman?"

"Yes."

"Do me a favor, then."

"What?"

"Don't get yourself killed."

"That is always uppermost in my mind, Eddie," Clint said.

Randle went back into the bank and Clint headed for Hannie's hotel.

Hannie got directions to Mrs. Buchanan's boardinghouse and, eventually, was standing right out in front of it. Her options were to storm in with her gun out, or to wait for Doyle to come outside. She didn't know how many other boarders there were, so she decided not to go in and risk a gun battle with innocent people getting hurt. She was surprised to find herself thinking this way. Up to now her anger had been burning so whitehot that she didn't care if innocent people got hurt.

Damn Clint Adams to hell.

• • •

When Clint found Hannie's room empty, he ran down to the desk clerk.

"Did you see Miss Welch leave?"

"Welch?" the young clerk asked.

"Room five?" Clint said. "Tall, lots of brown hair, pretty."

"Oh." The boy's eyes lit up. "Oh, yes, sir, I saw her leave just a little while ago."

"Any idea which way she went?"

"No, sir."

It didn't matter really. He was pretty sure she wasn't going to get breakfast.

"How do I get to the Buchanan boardinghouse?" he asked.

THIRTY-EIGHT

When Doyle finished his breakfast, he decided not to go back to his room. He walked to the front of the house and looked out the window. The tall woman wearing a gun was standing in the middle of the street, waiting.

He turned and went through the dining room, to the kitchen door.

"Mr. Doyle, I don't like my boarders to use the back door!" Mrs. Buchanan shouted.

He ignored her and went out the door.

Hannie was out front, getting impatient. She kept her eyes glued to the front door, waiting for it to open. She planned to draw and fire as soon as it did.

Clint was running down the street toward the boarding-house. When he came within sight of it, he could see Hannie standing on the street out front, waiting. Good, at least she hadn't gone rushing in.

He saw movement on one side of the house and quickened his pace.

• • •

Doyle snuck along the side of the house, and as he
approached the front, he drew his gun. He stopped at
the end of the wall and peered around. He had a clear
view of Hannie Welch, who was staring intently at
the front door.

This was going to be easy.

Hannie had no idea that Doyle was looking at her
from the cover of the wall of the house. She had no
idea that he was aiming his gun at her. She was still
staring at the front door, flexing her fingers, waiting
to draw her gun, waiting to end it. This would be the
last one, and then she'd take off the gun for good.

Clint was getting closer to Hannie, and he could see
the man with the gun alongside the house. This had
to be Doyle, and he was planning to cowardly shoot
her from ambush.

"Hannie! Watch out!"

Hannie heard Clint shout, but she didn't know which
way to look. In the end she turned her back to look
at him, giving Doyle a clear shot at a spot between
her shoulder blades.

When Doyle saw the woman turn, he stepped out
from behind the wall. He had not heard Clint Adams
call out to her. As intently as Hannie had been
looking at the front door, Doyle had been looking at
her.

Doyle cocked the hammer on his single-action

gun in preparation to firing. It was the time it took
him to cock it that saved her life.

In the time that it took Doyle to cock the hammer on
his gun, Clint drew and fired. His bullet struck Doyle
dead center in the chest, knocking the man back a
few steps before he fell to the ground.

Hannie Welch saw Clint draw and fire. If he hadn't
been so unbelievably fast, she might have drawn her
gun instinctively, but his speed gave her no time to
react by instinct.

She turned to see where his fired shot had gone,
saw the bullet hit Doyle, and saw the man go down.

"You all right?" Clint asked when he reached her,
even though Doyle had not fired.

"Yes," she said, "yes, I'm fine. W-what happened?"

"He was going to ambush you," Clint said.

"I–I didn't see him," she said. "I was concentrat-
ing on the front door."

"I know. Come on, let's take a look, make sure
he's your man."

They walked over to where the body was lying on
its back.

"Is that him?" Clint asked. "Is that the fourth
man?"

"That's him."

"Then it's over for you."

"It's over."

Clint looked up and saw a crowd forming in the
street, then saw the sheriff and his deputy coming toward them.

"Let me do the talking," he told her.

"All right."

Mort and Sam had spent the night sleeping on the floor in the storeroom. Thomas coming down from upstairs woke them up.

"Where's John?" Mort asked.

"He went out early," Thomas said. "I think he went looking for Doyle."

"To do what?"

"Try to get rid of him without killing him."

"Think that's gonna be possible?" Mort asked.

"I don't know—"

The front door slammed open and John came running in. "Looks like two of our problems got solved this mornin'," he shouted.

"How's that?" Thomas asked.

"Doyle's dead," John said. "That solves one problem."

"Who killed him?"

"That's what solves our other problem," John said. "It was the Gunsmith. Guess that's what he was doing in town. Now we're clear to go ahead."

"All we have to do is choose our target," Mort said.

With a big smile John said, "I think I got the answer to that, too."

THIRTY-NINE

Clint and Hannie left the sheriff's office.

"I thought he was going to lock me up," she said.

"No way," Clint said. "I'm the one who actually killed Doyle."

"I got locked up all the other times."

"But you pulled the trigger, right?"

"Yes."

He touched her arm.

"It's over, Hannie," he said. "You're free to continue your life."

"My life?" she asked. "I don't know what my life is. This has taken me two years, Clint. I don't have anything to go back to."

"Then you're going to have to figure that out."

She took a deep breath and let it out. "What are you gonna do now?"

"I've got something else to do."

"Somebody else to help?"

"Yes?"

"Could you use me?"

He looked at her. "You'd have to keep your gun on."

"I know."

"Can you use it?"

"I can."

"I might be able to use you," he said. "But I'll have to check with my . . . my other friend."

"Okay," she said. "I'll be around. I've got no place to go, nothing else to do."

"Why don't I come by your hotel later and we can get something to eat?"

"Okay."

"And I'll let you know if we can use you."

"Sure," she said. "I'm gonna stop at the saloon for a drink."

"Okay," he said. "I'm on my way there, so I'll have one with you."

She looked at him.

"Did I remember to say thank you for saving my life?" she asked.

He smiled. "I think I heard that."

"How much?" Mort asked.

"A hundred thousand dollars," John said.

The brothers exchanged a glance.

"A hundred thousand?" Sam asked in awe.

"What is it?" Thomas asked.

"It's supposed to be a federal payroll," John said.

"And it's already in the bank?" Mort asked.

"Yup."

"How did they do that?"

"During the night is what people are guessing."

"Federal payroll?" Thomas said again. "For what? There's no federal institution here."

"It's a stopover," John said.

"To where?"

"I don't know," John said. "All I know is that we have about three days to get it out of there."

"Now, wait, wait," Thomas said. His three brothers' excitement was mounting; he could feel it. "Let's think about this."

"What is there to think about?" John asked. "A hundred thousand. We could stop with that kind of money. We could leave Dexter."

"And go where?" Thomas asked.

"Who cares?" John asked.

"Hittin' a bank in our own town—" Thomas said.

"Tommy, what's the problem?" Sam asked. "It's not like we'd stay after, right?" He looked at his other brothers for support.

Somebody knocked on the front door.

"Forget it," Thomas said as John started for the front.

"We're supposed to be open," John said. "We don't want anythin' to look funny. Not if we're gonna do this."

"We don't know if we're gonna do it," Thomas said.

John looked at Mort.

"Go on, John," Mort said, "open the store."

John left the storeroom.

"Mort—"

"You wanna run this store forever, Tommy?" Mort asked. "Because I sure don't wanna work that farm for the rest of my life."

"Yeah, but—"

"This is the big hit we've been waitin' for."

"I didn't know we were waitin' for one big one."

"Then you ain't as smart as I thought you were," Mort said.

FORTY

"They're not open," Hannie said as they reached the Ox Bow.

"Don't worry," Clint said, "I have some pull."

He banged on the door until Sean Sanchez opened the door.

"Hey, Mr. Adams."

"Sean, can we come in?"

"We?" He looked past Clint and saw Hannie. His eyes widened. "Oh, sure, sure thing."

He backed away, allowed them to enter, then closed and locked the door. He was carrying his broom.

"Eddie ain't come down yet."

But right at that point they heard a door close upstairs and then Eddie Randle came down the stairs.

"Good mornin'," he said. "Is this the lady you been helpin' out?"

"This is Hannie Welch," Clint said. "We both kind of need a drink."

"Whiskey? Coffee?"

"A little of both would be good," Hannie said.

Randle poured three cups of coffee, then added a
slug of whiskey to each and carried them to a table.

"What's goin' on?" he asked when the three of
them were seated.

Clint told him how he had killed a man named
Frank Doyle that morning, how Doyle had been the
last of four men who has killed Hannie's sister.

"He tried to ambush her, but I got him first."

"So then we're drinkin' to celebrate?"

"I don't celebrate killing someone," Clint said.

"No, but she can celebrate the end of her hunt,"
Randle said, "and the beginning of the rest of her life."

"About that," Clint said, "she wants to help."

"Help?"

"She's got nothing else to do."

Randle leaned toward Clint.

"Have you . . . told her anythin'?"

"I haven't told her anything," Clint said.

"He just told me he's helpin' a friend," Hannie
said, "and I offered my help."

"And then she said she wanted a drink," Clint said,
"so I brought her here."

"Thanks for the business. Can we talk in my office?"

"Sure."

"Sean, make sure the lady gets whatever she wants,"
Randle said.

"Sure, Eddie."

Clint and Randle went into his office, where the
deputy marshal sat behind his desk.

"What's your pitch here?" Randle asked.

"We could use an extra gun."

"Is she any good?"

"She's killed three men, that I know of."

"Can we trust her?"

"Why not?"

Randle frowned. "We don't really need her."

"Fine," Clint said, "if you don't want to use her, we won't. You and I can spend all our time watching the bank."

"Okay, how much do you want to tell her?"

"Well, she'll probably wonder why we're doing this if we don't tell her you're a lawman."

Randle frowned again.

"Look at it this way," Clint said. "You get to take your badge out of the drawer again."

FORTY-ONE

"Is that real?" Hannie asked.

She was leaning over and looking at the deputy marshal's badge on the desk.

Randle looked insulted. He looked at Clint, who shrugged.

"Of course it's real."

She straightened.

"So what's the plan?" she asked.

"Have a seat," Randle said, "and we'll fill you in."

"What's the plan?" Sam asked.

Mort said, "Thomas will work out the plan tonight, after the store closes."

Mort and Sam were back at the farm, which looked even worse to Mort now that they were so close to leaving it.

"A hundred thousand dollars," Sam said. "That's a lot of money, Mort."

"Yep."

"How much is that each?"

"Twenty-five thousand."

"Twenty-five thousand dollars," Sam breathed.

"Sammy, stop repeating the amount all the time."

"Are we gonna stay together, Mort, or split up?"

"I don't know," Mort said. "I guess that'll be up to each of us."

"We're brothers," Sam said, "we should stay together."

"Yeah, well, we'll see about that."

Sam rubbed his hands together. "My first job. I can't wait."

"First," Mort said, "and last."

"So we're just gonna sit on the bank and wait for them?" Hannie asked.

"That's the plan."

"What makes you think they'll come?"

"A hundred thousand dollars," Randle said slowly. "They'll figure it's worth the risk." They had not told Hannie the whole story. She didn't know that the hundred thousand was a setup. "They're not afraid the sheriff will stop them?"

"No," Clint said, "I still think the sheriff is not what he seems. I think he knew Doyle."

"Can't prove that with Doyle dead," Randle said.

"No," Clint said, "we sure can't."

"I got an idea," Thomas said as he locked the front door hours later.

"What?" John asked.

"It's about the kid."

"Sammy?"

Thomas nodded and pulled the shades down on the windows.

"What about him?" John asked.

Thomas turned to face his brother.

"Why should he be in on this job?" he asked. "It's our last one."

"You mean . . . you wanna leave him behind?" John asked.

"We leave him at the farm, pull the job, then pick him up. He's free and clear, never pulled a job in his life."

"Mama would like that," John said.

"I know."

"You know we'll have to tie him up."

"Oh yeah," Thomas said.

Clint and Hannie lay on the bed in his hotel room. They had given hers up, and were talking things over.

"We'll take shifts in the bank, using the back door," Clint said. "One of us inside, two outside."

"I just had a thought."

"What?"

She propped herself up on an elbow and looked at him.

"What if somebody else rises to the bait?" she asked. "What if somebody else tries to rob the bank?"

"Let's hope that doesn't happen," Clint said. "If it does, we'd be back at square one, trying to find evidence on the Archers."

"We? Why not the deputy marshal?"

"Well, I agreed to help him catch them," Clint said. "I wouldn't be able to back out on him."

"You're an honorable man."

She settled back into his shoulder.

"After those four men killed my sister—well,

even before that—I didn't have a very high opinion of men."

"And now?"

She hesitated, then said, "Well, I have a high opinion of you. I guess that's a start."

FORTY-TWO

The next morning Thomas and John rode out to the farm for breakfast.

"We'll hit the bank today," Thomas said. "Why wait?"

"Great!" Sam said.

John took some more flapjacks and doused them with syrup.

"Mort, what do you want to do about the farm?" he asked.

"Leave it."

"And the store, Tommy?"

"Leave it," Thomas said. "We hit the bank and keep on goin'."

"To where?" Sam asked.

"Mexico," Thomas said. "We'll lay low there for a few years."

"Years?" Sam asked.

"This is not the kind of bank robbery that's gonna be forgotten anytime soon, Sammy," John said. "We'll have to stay in Mexico at least a few years until things blow over."

"Well," Sam said, "do they take American money in Mexico?"

"They love American money in Mexico," Thomas told him. "Come on, Sammy. Eat up. You're gonna need your strength."

Clint answered the knock on his hotel room door. Hannie and he were dressed and already wearing their guns.

"Morning, Beau," Clint said to the liveryman.

"They rode out of here early, Mr. Adams."

"Who did?"

"Thomas and John Archer," Beau said. "They keep their horses at my place."

"I didn't know that," Clint said.

"Yeah," Beau said, "when their brothers hassled me, I don't think they knew either."

"Okay, Beau, thanks."

Because it was early, Eddie Randle answered the pounding on the front door himself. Sanchez hadn't come by yet to sweep.

"What the hell—" he said when he saw Clint and Hannie.

"The Archers rode out this morning," Clint said.

"Out?"

"Probably out to the farm to get the other two," Clint said. "They're going to do it today."

The deputy marshal rubbed his face vigorously.

"Okay," he said, "we better get into place."

"Okay," Mort said, "I guess we better get goin'."

"Just one thing," Thomas said, nodding to brother John.

They both grabbed Sam and pinned his arms to the chair. Thomas looped a rope around their younger brother, who was struggling and yelling.

"What are ya doin'?"

Mort watched. He hadn't been in on the plan, but he caught on pretty quick.

"Don't worry, Sammy," he said. "When we come back with the money, we'll untie you."

FORTY-THREE

When the three Archers rode into town, nobody paid them any mind. They were part of the town landscape. Why should their arrival arouse any interest or suspicion?

They reined in their horses in front of the bank and dismounted. They had already decided that they would all go inside. Leaving one brother outside would look odd.

When they entered, none of the patrons, tellers, or other employees thought anything of it. Just three of the Archer boys coming into the bank.

Things were going according to plan.

But once inside, things changed . . . for everyone.

Thomas, John, and Mort all drew their guns.

"Ladies and gents," Thomas said, "please don't be alarmed. If everyone does what they're told, no one will get hurt."

For a moment their neighbors thought they were joking.

"Hey, Johnny," a teller named Rickert asked, "what's goin' on?"

"Mr. Rickert," John said, "we come for the federal payroll. If we gets it, nobody gets hurt."

"Payroll?" Rickert asked. He was the head teller, a mousy man of forty-five or so. He had been held up twice before, in other jobs. "What federal payroll?"

"Don't fool around," Thomas said. "The hundred thousand dollars."

Rickert looked even more puzzled.

"John, if there was a hundred thousand dollars in this bank, I'd know about it."

Thomas came over to the head teller's window and stood next to John. Mort kept the other people covered.

"Where's the manager? Where's Mr. Morris?"

"H-he's in his office."

"I'll check," Thomas said to Mort and John. "If anyone tries anything, kill 'em."

Suddenly, Mr. Rickert knew this was dead serious, but there was nothing he could do to warn Mr. Morris.

Thomas moved around behind the head teller's window, approached the door to the manager's office, and opened it without knocking. He found himself looking down the barrel of Clint Adams's gun.

"Don't move," Clint said, "don't even breathe."

Outside the bank, as soon as the Archers entered, Deputy Marshal Eddie Reed and Hannie Welch had approached the bank and watched through the windows. As soon as Thomas went to the manager's office, Reed said, "We make our move now."

"Why don't we wait for them to come out?" Hannie asked.

"No," Reed said, "somebody inside might get hurt. Let's go. You follow me in."

The deputy walked to the door and slammed it open. He stepped inside and said, "Drop your guns, boys!"

He felt the cold circle of the end of a gun barrel press against the back of his head.

"No, Deputy," Hannie said, "you drop your gun."

"We have a Mexican standoff, Adams," Thomas said.

"How do you figure?"

"My girl's got her gun to your deputy's head."

"What are you talking—" Clint stopped short when he realized there was only one thing this could have meant. "Crap."

"Now you've got it."

"You brought her in—"

"—to take care of Doyle."

"So her whole story?"

"Phony," Thomas said. "She likes stories."

"Your brothers, they knew?"

"They don't know everything I know," Thomas said, "or everyone I know."

"I see."

"Let's see . . . Hannie?" he called out.

"I've got him!"

"Stand by!" Thomas said.

At that moment Clint was glad they hadn't told Hannie that the payroll was phony.

"Thomas," Clint said, "listen carefully. There is no payroll."

"You're lyin'."

"No, it was a trick to draw you and your brothers out," Clint said. "Think about it."

Thomas did think about it, and it made him angry.

"Son of a bitch," he swore.

"Now which one of us feels more stupid?"

They marched the Archers and Hannie Welch out of the bank at gunpoint, both Clint and Deputy Marshal Reed shocked that Sheriff Perry had come up behind Hannie Welch and pressed his gun to *her* head.

"I may not be the straightest arrow who ever wore a badge," Perry said to them, "but I'll be damned if I'm gonna let anybody rob the bank in my town."

"You might want to send your deputy out to the Archer farm," Clint said. "Apparently they left little brother there."

"I'll take care of it."

"I'll be along in a minute, Sheriff," Reed said.

"Okay, Deputy."

As Perry walked the Archers and Hannie to the jail, Clint said, "Thomas was afraid they'd hang for their last job."

"If we can prove they've been behind all those jobs, yeah, they will hang," Deputy Marshal Reed said. He put his hand out for Clint to shake. "Thanks for helpin' me wrap this up."

"What are you going to do with the saloon now?" Clint asked.

Reed shrugged.

"Get rid of it."

"What about giving it to Newly?"

"Newly's not the simple bartender you think he is," Reed said. "He's workin' his own angles, so I'm not about to hand him anythin'. I could sell it, but the money would have to go to Uncle Sam. What are you gonna do?"

"Me? I'm headed back to the other side of the Mississippi," Clint said. "No good ever comes from being east of the river."

Watch for

THE DUBLIN DETECTIVE

329th novel in the exciting GUNSMITH series
from Jove

Coming in May!

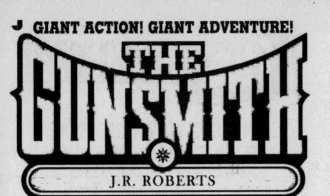

GIANT ACTION! GIANT ADVENTURE!

THE Gunsmith

J.R. ROBERTS

Little Sureshot And
The Wild West Show
(Gunsmith Giant #9)

Dead Weight
(Gunsmith Giant #10)

Red Mountain
(Gunsmith Giant #11)

The Knights of Misery
(Gunsmith Giant #12)

The Marshal from Paris
(Gunsmith Giant #13)

penguin.com/actionwesterns

M228AS0808

GIANT-SIZED ADVENTURE FROM AVENGING ANGEL LONGARM.

BY TABOR EVANS

2006 Giant Edition:

LONGARM AND THE OUTLAW EMPRESS

2007 Giant Edition:

LONGARM AND THE GOLDEN EAGLE SHOOT-OUT

2008 Giant Edition:

LONGARM AND THE VALLEY OF SKULLS

penguin.com/actionwesterns